Amor Vin[cit]
an Andrew Val[o]

Keith Massey

Lingua Sacra Publishing
Roxbury, New Jersey

Amor Vincit Omnia: an Andrew Valquist Adventure
Copyright © 2012 by Keith Massey

All rights reserved.
Published in the United States by Lingua Sacra Publishing.
www.linguasacrapublishing.com
ISBN 978-0-9843432-8-7

Dedication

To Archpriest John Kassatkin and Matushka Maxine, faithful servants of God. Многая лета! May God grant them many years!

About the Author

Keith Massey, Ph.D., is the author of *Intermediate Arabic for Dummies, Next Stop: Spanish, A Place of Brightness,* and *In Saecula Saeculorum.* He is a former linguist with the National Security Agency and is currently a language instructor.

Legal Disclaimer

The views and opinions expressed in this work are the author's and not those of the National Security Agency or the U.S. Government.

The Security Office of the National Security Agency reviewed this manuscript and ordered the deletion of some material. That material was removed and the NSA has stated that in the current book "NSA/CSS equities are protected."

Chapter One

Monday, March 14, 2005

The day had finally arrived! I stood in a line of people at the National Security Agency's Friendship Annex (which they depersonalize and call the FANX). I had been told to bring a copy of my birth certificate and two picture IDs. The line of new employees stretched outside. I could see my breath on that chilly spring morning.

"I can't wait to come in from the cold," I joked to a man behind me in line.

He didn't respond, apparently unaware of the spy craft jargon where "come in from the cold" means to return from an undercover assignment. (And, in that instant, I had no idea just how soon I would go abroad undercover.)

As I stood outside the door, waiting my turn for procedures I did not completely understand, I looked the FANX facilities over. Tall and presumably electrified barbed wire embraced several tan buildings. I had been inside this area twice before. This was the complex several miles north of the main NSA facilities at Fort Meade, Maryland. The FANX is used to process applicants for the various tests they need to take before being hired at the NSA. Not far from where I waited, I could see the two-story office building where I had taken my Arabic tests several months earlier.

They had flown me from Chicago, where I was staying with my twin brother Stefan and his family after I finished my tour in Iraq with the Army. The NSA put me up in a nearby hotel and gave me vouchers to eat in the restaurant there. For two days I took language tests, both reading skills and listening exercises in Arabic. Now, my Arabic was pretty good since it was part of my Ph.D. and I had spent a year speaking it regularly in Iraq. I passed those tests and I seemed to be on a fast track to get into the NSA.

That's when I hit a huge roadblock. My Top Secret (TS) security clearance was not so easy to get. Basically, for a TS, you have to be a United States citizen (check, I was born in Wisconsin). You also can't have any immediate family who aren't citizens (check, all I have is a twin brother, also born in Wisconsin). The other thing is, I had a Secret clearance when I was in the Army. And that's supposed to make getting TS all the more easy since they don't have to reinvestigate times you've already accounted for.

For a TS clearance, you need to describe where you were and with whom you were for the previous ten years. You see, they're always trying to disprove the unlikely hypothesis that you are secretly an agent of a foreign government's intelligence service. If such a person ever got a Top Secret clearance, you can imagine the security disaster that would be for us. So, if someone can't explain adequately where they were for an entire month two years ago, who knows? Maybe that was the month they spent in Russia being briefed by Russian Intelligence for a mission to be a deep mole.

But, why would this be difficult in my case, you wonder? Well, here's the problem. The day after getting back from Iraq, my twin brother and I went to Romania for a month, during which time we actually ended up working with the Romanian Secret Intelligence Agency SRI (*Serviciul Român de Informaţii*). It's a long and complicated story. It's a good story, but not something to be explained away in a single sentence on my security forms. (And it's a story told in the novel *A Place of Brightness*.)

After I sent in all the paperwork for my clearance, page after page, about forty in all, documenting my whereabouts for the previous ten years, I got a call for an interview with the Department of Defense investigator who would be researching me for a possible clearance. She had me meet her at the local post office. Apparently a DOD investigator can just call the local post office and say, "Hey, I need office space. Make it so."

She began asking a few follow-up questions based on the things I put in my forms. And then came the big one.

"Um, can you tell me more about this month in Romania earlier this year?"

I decided to tell the entire truth. The second I mentioned SRI she starts shaking her head.

"This may not be fixable, do you realize that?" she said.

And so began the longest six months of my life. I needed this job. I had no other decent prospects at the time. There simply aren't any jobs in higher education. Sure, I had a Ph.D., but so do a thousand other people. As it is, I ended up becoming a finalist for a position at a small liberal arts college in the Midwest. I had a Ph.D. completed, I had teaching experience, and I had academic publications in peer-reviewed journals. But I didn't get the job. I found out later that someone with just a Master's Degree, no teaching experience, and no publications got the position. Oh, and she was also the godchild of the college president. After that humiliation, I had no will left to send a resume to colleges, knowing that someone else out there already knew they had the job and the so-called search process was just a legal formality. Now, I had taught Latin in a high school before joining the Army. And I suppose I could have gone searching for a similar job elsewhere in the United States. But if I had to start all over again, I wanted it to be in something very fresh. And so, I had decided that, for the time being, this NSA thing was my best prospect.

But for six months I was told that the DOD was still looking into my possible connections to a foreign intelligence service and my clearance was in limbo. With each passing day I was more stressed out, thinking that my clearance might not happen at all. I remember that, in that timeframe, I got an email from someone claiming to be a Nigerian general with a business proposition and I was so paranoid that I called the FBI to report it, just in case this was a secret NSA test to see how I would react to such things.

While all that was still in process, the NSA scheduled me to do my polygraph test. Again they flew me to Washington and put me up at that same hotel. They told me to be ready to get on a bus the following morning to be taken to the FANX complex where the polygraph would take place.

Now, something unusual happened that night. I was in bed, in my hotel room, trying to relax in preparation for what I assumed would be a stressful next day. Then I heard a noise at the door. It's someone trying the knob. And then, the door opens!

Into my room walks a tall woman, early thirties, long blonde hair, quite—fit. She is apparently a flight attendant, judging from the smart blue dress-uniform and matching hat. And Baltimore-Washington International Airport was not far from this hotel.

She does not see me and puts her bag down on the dresser. I'm speechless, unable to imagine how she has gotten in here.

She turns and, upon seeing a man in the bed, shouts, "What are you doing here?!"

"This is my room!" I explain.

She sighs heavily. "This happens sometimes. They accidentally double book a room and reissue a key for it."

I'm still quite flustered. "I guess that's what happened."

Then she smiles at me and says, "You know, we could just share this place."

And it hits me. Of course this isn't happening! This is a test from the NSA! I mean, I'm here to complete security tests, including a lie detector. So they're setting up this scenario to determine how I would react to it. This is the stuff of fantasy. So this can't possibly be real.

"No, miss," I say loudly. "That is not going to happen. You need to leave--right now."

She looks at me dumbfounded and grabs her bag from the dresser. Then she turns in a huff, goes out the door, and slams it behind her.

Now, you know already that I will eventually go to work at the NSA. And after I had been there several weeks I went to the security office and asked about this incident. And I learned that the NSA does not do such tests.

That's right. It was real. It wasn't a test. I kicked a beautiful flight attendant out of my hotel room that night. Oh well, I guess I'm sure it was for the best. (Though I admit I revisit the incident in my mind from time to time.)

The next morning, I arrived at the FANX for my polygraph. Obviously I'm nervous. I mean, I've never had a lie-detector test before. A bunch of us are sitting there waiting our turn. We're in the same large room where I had hung out some months before while waiting between language tests. It's like an airport lobby, short gray carpet, dozens of benches facing each other. Televisions in every corner of the room displayed the latest news, as if implying that the NSA already knew everything projected there last Tuesday. They also have a nice coffee service. As I drink several cups, I can feel my stress level rising. In retrospect, you probably shouldn't drink too much coffee before a polygraph test, but who tells you these things?

I see official looking people entering the waiting room and calling out names. Judging from the agency badges worn by most of the people waiting, there were more current employees being re-polygraphed than first timers seeking employment. I would later learn that you have to be retested every five years.

"Jenn Roher?" a man asks.

A woman near me stands and approaches him. I see them shake hands and he leads her down a foreboding hallway.

It feels like an eternity. I drink more coffee.

"Andrew Valquist?" I hear.

Standing from my chair, I approach a tall blue-suited and gray-haired man.

"I'm Stan. I'll be your polygrapher today."

I shake his hand and off we go.

We enter a small room with a massive mirror I assumed to be a one-way window. Bright florescent lights shone from the ceiling against the other walls, all sporting cream-colored panels. Things seem just very polite until he starts putting "The Equipment" on me. A blood pressure cuff goes on my right arm. On the other hand he puts a little metal cup over my index finger (to measure perspiration). And then he puts yards of what look like curled old-style telephone cords around my chest (to measure my breathing).

"Are you comfortable?"

"Yes," I lie. And it occurs to me that my lie detector test is officially off to a poor start.

"Just relax and answer everything I ask as truthfully as you can."

"Yes, sir."

I was immediately put at ease by the fact that the questions were no-brainers.

"Are you Andrew Valquist?"

"Yes," I said truthfully.

Now, in retrospect, it's not irrelevant to ask a man with an identical twin if he really is the person he claims to be.

But then the questions got harder.

"Have you ever taken illegal drugs?"

I started to explain the circumstances behind a single ill-advised puff on a joint at a party in high school where there was this really fantastic red-head I was trying to...

"Yes or no!" he snapped.

His tone took me by surprise.

"Yes," I said.

"Have you ever *sold* illegal drugs?"

"No," I said, truthfully.

Soon came the questions I was dreading the most.

"Are you now or have you ever been a member of an organization which intends the overthrow of the United States government?"

"No."

"Are you now or have you ever been employed by a foreign government?"

I decided in that instant that he obviously was not willing to hear the complicated explanation of why I had worked *with*—but not *for*— the SRI several months earlier. And the real purpose of this question was to find out if I was an undercover plant secretly working for a foreign intelligence agency, which I was not.

"No," I said, feeling my blood pressure spike at the ambiguity of my situation.

He fell silent, and began writing several notes on his clipboard. After what seemed an eternity, he pulled his chair directly in front of mine. He leaned into me so close that I could smell every seeping and stinking cavity in his teeth.

"You're lying to me," he said loudly.

I was in shock. "No, I'm not," I finally offered.

"Yes, you are," he returned. "When you said you've never sold illegal drugs, I can tell you're lying. And you are not going to leave this room until you admit the truth."

Wow, I thought. That's one point on which I am quite sure. I really never have sold illegal drugs. I've never sold *legal* drugs. I've actually never sold *anything*. Now, I knew my answer to the question about foreign governments was a matter of interpretation. And my DOD investigator knew the whole story and was out there trying to sort all that out. Even so, I was surprised that the machine saw me as evasive on this particular question.

"It's one o'clock right now," he said. "I've got nowhere to go. You will not leave this room until you admit that you have sold illegal drugs."

And so, the showdown began. An eternity of silence went by. I don't know exactly how long. It felt like hours but I think in the end it was something on the order of fifteen minutes.

"You really aren't leaving here until you admit it," he said.

"I've never sold illegal drugs," I repeated.

He shook his head. Getting up from his chair, he began to remove "The Equipment."

"Get out of here," he said in disgust.

I walked out the door, my heart falling and believing that this opportunity was now lost.

A man in a black suit stopped me as I entered the waiting room. "Dr. Valquist?" he said. "Go back to your hotel room and relax. We're rescheduling you for another polygraph tomorrow."

"What?" I said bewildered. "I thought I failed it!"

"A lot of people fail it the first time. Just relax and we'll try this again tomorrow."

Back at my hotel room, I tried to make sense of the day. I concluded that, for whatever reason, I must have unconsciously projected anxiety from one question into another where it simply didn't belong. And I also learned later that they don't intentionally mess with people in a polygraph just to see how they will respond.

The following morning, I breezed through my second polygraph. I had a different examiner, which is their policy. And the man told me as he unhooked "The Equipment" that he would have repeated questions a second time if there were a problem. That was as close as he could come to telling me I passed.

Five months later I got an email informing me that I had my TS clearance. And I learned that my EOD (Entry On Duty) date was March 14, which was still a ways off.

I'm not going to go into depth on the bittersweet time that followed with my brother and his family. We had drifted apart when I went to grad school and he went to seminary. (He's an Eastern Orthodox priest today.) And then I was in the Army and went to Iraq. But now we had just finished several months together, which included an adventure in Romania we could never have anticipated. Anyway, I said I wasn't going to go into depth on it, so it'll suffice to say that tears were shed and plenty of wine was drunk.

I moved everything I owned, which all fit in my car, to a one-bedroom apartment just west of Fort Meade,

Maryland, the Army base which houses the main campus of the National Security Agency.

And that brings me back finally to the long row of people on a crisp spring morning at the FANX. My turn arrived, I presented my papers, they confirmed my name on their lists, and I sat for my ID picture. The group of us, about fifty in all, were taken from room to room that morning for what seemed like endless human resource information sessions.

After a lunch in the FANX cafeteria (where I had eaten for free when I came for the language tests and polygraph, but this time had to pay), we were all put on a bus for the main NSA complex at Fort Meade. There was just one order of business left for the day. Just off the main hallway which connects Operations Buildings 1 and 2, we entered the main security briefing room. (I have heard this is the longest hallway in the country, if not the world.) As I stepped through the door, I was handed a manila envelope with my name printed on a white label. I took a seat in the front row and looked inside. There I found a plastic ID card, about the size of a driver's license. The picture they took of me earlier was printed on it. I now had an official agency badge.

Included with the agency badge was a chain to hang it on because we were required now to wear this thing around our necks to prove our right to be in a classified area. The only other thing in the folder was a single piece of paper. It was a pretty straightforward document. It explained that I, with a place to sign my assent to the terms, accepted a lifetime obligation to never divulge anything I learned that is classified and also to submit anything I write for pre-publication review, even if I leave the agency. Since leaving the NSA to become headmaster at the Fairfax Classical Academy, I've published academic articles with no Arabic content at all. It doesn't matter. I have to send them off to the NSA for review, just in case I even inadvertently mention something classified. (Adventures connected to my job at the Fairfax Classical Academy are described in the novel *In Saecula Saeculorum*.)

The briefing room was like a college lecture hall. Dark blue walls framed twenty rows of seats all facing a stage with a black podium sporting the NSA Seal, a Bald Eagle holding keys in its feet, ringed with the name of the Agency.

"Would everyone please rise," a woman at the front of the room said.

We all complied and a man in a black suit entered.

She introduced the man and described his rank and position within the NSA in a way that certainly sounded very high up the chain of command but which was utterly lost on me at the moment.

"I'm happy to have the opportunity to conduct your official swearing-in ceremony this morning," he said. "Please raise your right hand and repeat after me."

Now, that was not the first time I had raised my right hand and sworn to support and defend the Constitution of the United States against all enemies, foreign and domestic. But I am proud to add that the gentleman who swore me into the NSA that day would go on a few years later to attain the highest civilian office of the organization. He would eventually rise to the rank of Deputy Director, a position always held by a civilian. The Director himself is always a military officer at the four star general rank. I would go on to meet the Director in circumstances that I'll describe a bit later, though the details will have to be well-sanitized of certain classified points. Let's just say that embassies were closed, I was responsible, and, in retrospect, I was wrong.

That night, as I relaxed in my little apartment on the futon that also served as my bed, I sipped a glass of wine and looked at my badge. Greater adventures lay ahead of me than I could have imagined at that moment. And I certainly could not have imagined that those adventures would start the following morning.

Chapter Two

Tuesday, March 15

    My alarm jolted me from a fitful sleep at 6:00 AM. Before going to sleep, I'd spoken with my twin, Fr. Stefan Valquist, for a few hours on the phone, while we both refilled our wine glasses multiple times. As I lingered in bed for a few moments, I realized that I didn't even deserve to feel as good as I did.

    Following my normal morning ritual, I drank coffee and read the news on the Internet. After a quick shower, I headed toward the FANX where orientation would continue for a second day.

    One of the other new employees, Gregory, also an Arabic linguist, had been frustrated the previous day about how long the in-processing was taking. I had assured him that all these human resource briefings were legally necessary, and that we should cherish this down-time while we still could. I knew from my experience in the Army that the day would soon enough come when we would feel taxed mentally and physically in this line of work. We deserved to remember with fondness the simple salad days of orientation.

    I suppose that's easy for me to say. I mean, here Gregory's just all excited to "get in the fight." I had already been in the fight. I'd been to Iraq and I had helped bring down a neo-communist terror group in Romania right after that. So, I did understand where he was coming from. And the fact is, six months later Gregory had experienced more than his share of adventures.

So, I parked my car in the large lot across the street from the FANX and walked toward the orientation center for what I believed would be a boring day of briefings. I even craved it. I was actually looking forward to learning details about the matching funds in the government-sponsored retirement program.

But I would not get my wish.

And I was particularly looking forward to lunch in the FANX cafeteria that day. From my previous times there, testing for language and the polygraph debacle, I had learned that if it's Tuesday, it's Taco Salad Day!

And what a Taco Salad. A crunchy flaky bowl, ample meat, fresh and crispy lettuce. This was indeed going to be a great day.

I saw Gregory already seated in the orientation hall and took a place next to him. It was like a little theater, with two aisles running up the sides. I lowered the desk attached to the seat in front of me and started looking through papers in my orientation folder.

"Day Two!" I said. "I'm thinking of signing up for the medium risk retirement portfolio. How about you?"

"Good Lord!" he said, putting his head in his hands. "This is all so boring. I just want to get to my first assignment so I can start catching terrorists!"

"Your day will come, Gregory," I said. "But try to enjoy this time for what it is. You know about the Taco Salad, right?"

A phone at the front of the room screamed for attention. The woman conducting our orientation had been looking over some notes for the first briefing and went to answer it.

I saw her nodding and then looking into the crowd of new employees. When she spotted me, she suddenly smiled and hung up the phone.

"Dr. Valquist?" she said, walking quickly up the aisle. "A car is waiting outside the perimeter to pick you up."

"What's this about?" Gregory asked.

"I don't know."

"I don't either," she said. "But get going. They were very insistent."

I stood and left the room, suspecting that my Taco Salad was in serious jeopardy.

***

A black limousine was idling just outside the security perimeter as I walked back out the checkpoint.

"Short day for you, huh?" the guard asked.

I smiled. "Apparently I'm being summoned."

His face fell. "Good luck, sir."

I looked at him curiously as I stepped toward the vehicle. The door opened.

"Dr. Valquist?" a voice shouted. "Get in!"

I hopped into the car and was thrown against the back seat by the sudden acceleration.

"Wait!" I protested. "Can I get my seat belt on, please?"

Only then I spotted a man in a black suit seated across from me.

"The name's Hollings," he said, holding out his hand. "I'm your new boss."

As I shook his hand, I studied his face. He was balding with brown hair, heavy set, with red blotchy skin.

"This is a summary of what we're about to discuss," he said, handing me a manila folder. "You can read it more on the plane."

We sped south down the Baltimore-Washington Parkway at well above the speed limit, compliments of a Maryland State Police escort blaring its sirens all around us.

"Apparently I'm flying somewhere?" I asked. "Can you tell me a little more?"

"We're on our way to Andrews Air Force Base, where you're getting on a flight to Constanța."

"Constanța? As in Constanța, Romania?"

"Yes. You've been there?"

"No, only Bucharest and Brașov. What's in Constanța?"

"A US Air Force base. Your ride can only land there."

I sat back in my seat and tried to process all I had heard. "There must be a mistake," I said. "I'm an Arabic linguist. And I didn't think that the NSA did clandestine missions. Isn't that more of a CIA thing?"

He chuckled. "Most NSA employees don't even know about the division you're now working for."

"And I get to find out my second day on the job?" I asked. "I assume you need someone who can speak Romanian? That's why I'm being selected."

"That's helpful," he said. "But it's primarily your knowledge of Latin that brought you to our attention."

"How could Latin matter to the NSA in the 21st century?"

"You're only going to learn this mission one step at a time," Hollings said. "After you land at our base, you'll be driven in a diplomatic car to Bucharest."

"Good. Now that's a city I know well. I was there about a year ago."

"We know all about that. You'll check into the Intercontinental and wait for further instructions."

I surveyed notes that said little more than what he had already told me. We entered Andrews AFB and sped into the runway area.

"One more question," I said. "Just how urgent is this mission?"

Hollings said nothing and I had my answer as we pulled up alongside a plane.

My mouth fell open as I looked out the window at an SR-71 Blackbird, a sleek spy plane I knew was capable of flying over Mach 3. There would be no reason to fly me to Romania in this thing unless they needed to move me at hypersonic speed.

"Pretty urgent, I guess."

"Quite," he said.

Chapter Three

Tuesday, March 15: 10:20 PM

"I have a reservation," I said, putting my passport on the black marble counter.

The woman there looked at my document and then typed on her computer. "Yes, sir, I have you booked for three nights with us," she said. "And it's already paid for." She was a typical Romanian woman. Tall, slender, and with the impossibly high cheek bones that make Eastern European women despised by their Western counterparts.

As she fluttered her fingers over the keyboard, I turned to survey the lobby. A bellhop stood a few yards from me, patiently waiting with a cart and my several large suitcases, which were filled with God knows what since they also weren't really mine. A dazzling cream floor reflected rich reddish-brown wood paneled walls. The place was sure a lot nicer than the hotel my twin and I stayed in a year earlier. At that time we were travelling on the salaries of an unemployed former soldier and an Orthodox priest. Even though I'd been told that my room was already been paid for, I just had to know how much this was costing the taxpayers.

"You're all set, sir," she said, handing me a pamphlet with my key cards. "You're in 732, a Junior Suite, King-sized bed, with a view on the square."

"How much is the room again?"

"279 Euros."

"What's that per night?" I asked.

"That *is* per night, sir."

Now, I'm not good at math, but I do know that if a dollar buys you about 75 Euro cents—well, that's a lot of money.

"*Mulţumesc frumos*," I said politely, putting an American accent in my words.

"*Cu plăcere*," she chimed back, with a bow.

The bellhop, my mysterious luggage, and I rode the elevator up to my room. I tipped him and I was finally alone.

It was 10:30 PM, Bucharest time. My mind swirled through the previous hours. At nine in the morning I got in the second seat of an SR-71 Blackbird. Now, while that plane can hit Mach 3, the pilot told me that we cruised at just over Mach 2 most of the trip, dropping down only for an in-air refueling somewhere just west of Great Britain. The SR-71 had been officially retired ten years ago, but the pilot explained that a couple are kept operational for what he called "exceptional situations requiring rapid personnel transport." I assumed that's a technical way of saying

"We have a spy in Washington who just has to be in Eastern Europe in four hours." And that's about how long it took.

Upon landing, another black-suited man met me just out of the plane.

"Dr. Valquist," he had said loudly, speaking over the roar of jet engines all around. "Where's your cell phone?"

"Still in my car back at the FANX parking lot." (We're not allowed to bring personal cell phones into NSA facilities.)

He chuckled. "Of course. Here's a replacement for your use on this mission."

I took the phone and touched the screen. "I've wanted one of these things! When do I learn what this mission is?"

"Check in to the Intercontinental in Bucharest and await further instructions."

A dark blue SUV approached.

"Here comes your ride. Good luck, sir."

A two hour drive on one of Romania's better highways had me at the Intercontinental Hotel in Bucharest, in my room, awaiting further instructions. It was only then that I realized I was ravenously hungry. I've experienced jetlag before. It can mess with your system. But this was a strange situation. Everything around me, the clock, the darkness outside, told me it was 10:30 PM. But I was sitting in the strength of my morning coffee at a conference room in Maryland just six hours earlier. I'd basically missed only one meal, but my brain was screaming at me as if I'd missed two.

On the desk in my hotel room was a menu in a dignified brown leather jacket. Nice touch, Intercontinental! I picked up the phone and dialed room service.

"*Da?*" I heard on the other end.

I ordered fast and furiously. A steak, yes. All the fixings and trimmings, yes. Oh, pair that with a bottle of *Comoara Pivniței*, a very fine red wine I had enjoyed here before. I mean, it's not "*Mediat*" for nothing!

I hung up the phone and collapsed into the bed...and...realized...I had just conducted the entire transaction in fluent Romanian.

Earlier I had used a mere courtesy phrase you could find on the first page of a guide-book. And then I spoke Romanian as if I had been raised by a Romanian defector who trained me to speak her native language and Russian so that I could come back to liberate the country from the godless Communists. (That's my background, by the way.)

I imagined the worst-case scenarios. The person who takes the orders for room service is speaking to the woman who checked me in. "Hey, that American in 732 sure does speak Romanian well." "No he doesn't! He barely managed 'Thank you'." Hmm... Someone was tricked, and it probably wasn't the one who heard fluent Romanian. "There's something funny going on here. We'd better call the police."

Settle down, Andrew. That's probably not going to happen. But be a little more careful next time.

And that's when it caught up to me. Here I was, in the field on some kind of mission I still didn't understand. And I was never given any briefings or training on what not to do. I assumed (and I was right) that the Intelligence Agencies have classes you are required to take before going into the field. I later learned that those classes were a chance to eat lunch in the fantastic food court the CIA has right inside their headquarters. I mean, the NSA Taco Salad I didn't get today is mighty fine, but the CIA has it all! They have a McDonalds. They have a Subway, Chinese, Mexican.

I heard a knock at the door. Opening it, I hoped to see a faster than anticipated cart with dinner dishes. Instead, though not unexpectedly, I saw a man in a black suit, a large manila envelope under his arm.

"I've kind of been expecting you," I said. "Come on in."

"*Mulțumesc*," he said in only slightly accented Romanian.

"*Cu plăcere*," I returned.

I took a seat in one of the lavishly upholstered chairs and pointed to the other. He joined me and handed me the envelope.

"In there is everything you need and everything you need to know for your mission tomorrow morning."

"Thank God it's tomorrow morning," I said. "I was worried that you might be sending me out in the middle of the night. Even though my body thinks it's three in the afternoon, I'd like some sleep pretty soon."

I opened the envelope and found a single sheet of paper and a little blue cardboard folder, just three by two inches. Embossed on the cover were the letters BNR. I opened the thing and saw my photograph on the left side. *Permis de Intrare*, Entrance Permit. And BNR turned out to be *Biblioteca Națională A României*.

"This is a library entrance pass for the Romanian National Library."

"Yes," he said. "That's where your mission tomorrow will take place."

"I've been flown to Romania in an SR-71 at Mach 2 to go a library in the morning? I need more. Please."

"I can tell you what the sheet of paper says," he began. "Your mission is to extract a particular book. It's just been catalogued and we believe it should be currently sitting on the third floor. Sometime tomorrow afternoon, we believe it will be put back in the book stacks, though we don't know where it might be filed."

I looked at the sheet of paper and saw sentences basically stating what he had just said. Then I found the title of the book: *De Economia Orbis Terrarum*.

"Concerning the Economy of the World?" I asked. "This is obviously a work written in Latin maybe just a few hundred years ago. I know for a fact that the word '*Economia*' with the meaning 'Economy' is not attested until about 1440 when…"

"Very good, Dr. Valquist," he interrupted. "We obviously have the right man for the job."

"You don't need someone who knows this background to find a book," I countered. "The title is probably visible on the cover. Any clandestine agent with some Romanian skills could do this thing. Why me?"

"You sell yourself short," he said. "The last thing we need is for some non-Latinist agent to bring us back a book that was mislabeled in the cataloguing office. We need someone who can find that book, absolutely confirm beyond a shadow of a doubt that he's got it, and then get it out of that library."

"Why is that the last thing you need?" I asked. "If that happened, couldn't you just send that agent, or another agent, back in to get the book in question?"

The man looked at me without responding.

"Wait," I said. "I get it. It's because there's some competition here. Someone else may be trying to get to that book as well. And that's why you had to fly *me* here at Mach 2. You know that I not only speak Romanian and know Latin, but I can also put up a fight if I need to. You believe that if we don't get this book tomorrow, someone else could end up with the thing. And you really don't want that to happen."

He nodded. "You're a very smart man, Dr. Valquist. I'm not cleared to tell you more. But I do feel the obligation to tell you that your instincts are correct. And for that reason, be very careful in there tomorrow."

I put the paper on the desk. "Let's assume I find the book and get it out of there. What next?"

"The moment you leave the library, we will know it. Work your way to the Lipscani neighborhood. It's just south from..."

"I know where it is," I interrupted.

"An agent will relieve you of the book there," he said.

I took a deep breath and slowly released it. "And there was really no other agent in the entire United States Intelligence Community that was capable of this mission besides a man in day two of orientation at the NSA?"

"We needed a competent Latinist who also spoke Romanian and who could fight if necessary. You assume we have seven of those?"

I chuckled. "Will you join me for dinner?"

"No," he said, getting up from his chair. "I have to go now. As the instructions state, the library opens at nine. Good luck."

He left my hotel room and immediately after I heard another knock at the door.

I opened to see the long awaited cart of dishes.

"Come in, my good man," I said. "I've been expecting you."

Chapter Four

Wednesday, March 16: 6:00 AM

The wakeup call roused me from a fitful sleep. My body clock had refused to believe in Bucharest time the previous night. Despite the over-the-top excitement of a supersonic jet flight and then the consolation of what turned into the better part of two bottles of *Comoara Pivniței*, I had not slept until somewhere in the neighborhood of 3 AM local time. Even then, I had trouble falling back asleep after a dream that I was in Iraq and trying to flee from mortar fire but I couldn't run except in slow motion. Upon waking, I recalled that this classic nightmare is described in Homer's *Iliad*, but then I was so annoyed with myself that I couldn't recall the exact reference that I ended up spending fifteen minutes first figuring out how to go on the internet with my new phone and then finding the information. (*Iliad*, Book 22.199-201, by the way. Go check it out.)

I showered, which made me feel almost normal. Now, for some breakfast. If you get to know me better, you'll learn that I'm very much a people person. And I hate eating alone. That's why I asked that agent from the previous evening if he would join me for dinner. I didn't even get the guy's name, but I wanted his company for my meal. And that's why I decided that I didn't want to just order room-service. Off I went to explore the restaurants of the Intercontinental. I found a nice breakfast buffet, included in the price of my room (the least they could do!). And being able to see other humans while I ate made me feel more comfortable.

Now, most Eastern European buffets don't understand what Americans think breakfast should be. We expect a variety of cereals or, if you are so inclined, eggs, sausage, fried potatoes, etc. Not so in Eastern Europe. There you find a breakfast buffet usually means slices of cold meat and cheese, pickled salads, and, if you're lucky, maybe toast with jam.

I once stayed with a family from the Danube Delta region and learned that for those people there's no such thing as breakfast without a healthy glass of vodka. Now, you've already noticed, I like my wine. But I was a bit conflicted about drinking vodka before my morning coffee. (For the sake of politely accepting their hospitality, of course, I consumed what was put in front of me.)

Anyway, the Intercontinental was decidedly catering to the desires of the American and British businessmen who stay there. I had scrambled eggs, sausage links, hash browns, and plenty of coffee. I was ready to go steal a book.

Back in my room, I decided to check out the luggage. The library opened at 9 AM and it was at most a five minute walk from the hotel. I had a little while before I really had to go out the door to be there just shortly after opening. I unzipped the large black rolling suitcase first.

Inside I found bundles of random clothing that an American businessman would probably have along. Various toiletries were wrapped in smaller plastic bags. The other suitcase checked out similarly. And then, spilling the contents of the smaller carry-on bag out onto the bed, my heart froze. A Glock 9 millimeter handgun had bounced upon the mattress.

I picked up the weapon and pressed a button on the left side of the handle to release the clip. It slipped out the bottom and I caught it with my left hand. It was full. Instinctively, I pulled back on the barrel and saw an already chambered cartridge fly out of the side and fall onto the bed. The gun had been topped off and then the clip refilled for a total of eleven shots on this particular model. This was the way we were taught to do it in the military.

I slapped the clip into the gun and pulled back the barrel to chamber a shot. Then I removed the clip and topped it off again with the cartridge on the bed. The gun was back to its original state.

But if I was intended to take this gun with me on the mission, why did the briefer not tell me this last night? I looked back onto the single briefing sheet and saw nothing about going into that library packing.

So what was I supposed to do? He as much as told me that I could expect competition for that book. I was officially angry. Well, I'd been in war and didn't intend to face a potentially armed adversary at a disadvantage if I didn't have to. So I stuffed the pistol between my back and belt and pulled my shirt out to cover it.

It was time that I could head toward the library. As I looked around that hotel room, I felt a sudden panic. This is not what I thought I was signing on to when I joined the NSA. I'm a Ph.D. in Classics with a minor in Arabic. I thought I was going to be translating, I don't know, maybe emails or phone calls—who knew what the NSA was capable of? I sure didn't know even in that moment, since I hadn't finished orientation. And now, here I was in Bucharest, Romania with a Glock 9 millimeter and orders to go into a library and somehow steal a book. I could feel my heart pounding in my chest with such a force that I worried I might have a cardiac episode. I'd been in serious danger before. But that just doesn't matter. Being in danger doesn't make you feel more at ease the next time you can seriously contemplate the loss of your life. If anything it's just the opposite.

I confirmed that my key card was in my wallet. My library pass was in there as well. I was ready to go. I left the room and rode the elevator down to the ground floor. Trying to seem casual, I walked through the lobby and out the front doors of the hotel.

A bright morning sun stung my eyes. I saw a busy boulevard packed with cars straight ahead. Just to my left was Piața Universității, the University Square. It was really just an intersection of two major roads, but it held a subterranean mini-mall beneath, complete with a metro stop.

I approached an escalator heading down under the square. These underground thoroughfares are common in Bucharest. It's a city where pedestrians rule. And so they provide these subterranean crossings at most every major intersection. But even on smaller streets, if someone steps into the road at any spot, all traffic is expected to come to a stop, under penalty of a ticket.

As I traveled downward, I reminded myself to stand up straight, lest I show the obvious bulge of a weapon in my lower back. I arrived at the bottom and found the area much as I had seen it a year earlier. Which included, I had somehow forgotten, a McDonald's! I almost wished I'd come here for a sausage, egg, and cheese biscuit instead of the Intercontinental.

On the other side of the underground, I arrived at a broken escalator going up toward the opposite corner from where I descended. Walking on a stalled escalator somehow feels strange to me. I saw a set of stairs next to it and opted for the real thing.

I was more than half way to the library. Continuing south along the boulevard, I passed a palatial white house surrounded by a tall wrought iron fence. It looked to be late 19th century, now converted into an art gallery. These types of buildings have become a rarity in Bucharest, replaced during Communism with blocs of cement flats that looked run down the year they were built. But before Communism, Bucharest was called the Paris of the East.

At the first street, I turned right and could already see the library just two blocks away. The roof was graced with tin tiles that sparkled in the morning sun. It's an impressive five story neoclassical structure, built from brown stone. It sits in the financial district of Bucharest because, prior to Communism, it was the stock exchange (but since they didn't need one of those anymore, they made it into the national library).

I walked quickly. On my right I passed an outdoor café. Across the street on my left was a movie theater showing a fairly current American film. It struck me that, under different circumstances, this might be one of my favorite streets in Bucharest. I've got a place to have a drink, catch a show, explore a library and...

Then just past the theater I saw a patch of green. Whatever this was, the buildings around it made it invisible from that main boulevard. I just had to see what was in this little arboretum. As I crossed the street toward it, I saw Russian-style church onion domes creep out over the trees. My heart surged. It was a Church. I needed this so badly. Just to be able to center myself before all the uncertainty.

The Communists had intentionally built up around churches in an attempt to hide them and marginalize religion in Romanian culture. This one was set back twenty feet in its courtyard, which meant that putting new buildings flush up to the church fence effectively obliterated it from view. Now, you might ask if the Communists were willing to go to such lengths to suppress religion, why not just go all the way? Why was this church and all the others not demolished? Well, the fact is, the Communists knew that the traditional sensibilities of the people could only be pushed so far and so fast. They had a long term plan to kill the Church with malign neglect. When a church needed repair, that was made difficult. When a church needed to be replaced, that was not allowed.

I crossed the street, walked quickly through the courtyard, and entered the church. Inside, I found a completely unlit hallway. I waited a moment for my eyes to adjust. Straight ahead, I saw a little booth with a glass window splattered with prayer cards. Inside, there was a nun dressed all in black, sitting and ready to sell candles, cards, and books to any visitor. Passing by her, I found the entrance to the sanctuary on my left.

I made the sign of the cross as I stepped over a wooden beam set in the floor. The church was tiny. Even packed with worshipers, this place could hold maybe a hundred people. As my eyes adjusted to the dim light produced only by stray candles, I saw the icons of saints and scenes from the Bible painted on every inch of the walls. It was wrong to bring a gun in here, I knew. But I had no choice. God forgive me that and all my other many sins. I walked up to the front of the Church and leaned over to kiss a central icon of Jesus, set in a stand just to right of the towering wall separating the congregation from the priest's altar.

"I don't ask your blessing on my mission," I whispered. "I only ask you to protect me."

As I walked out, I paused at the entrance of the sanctuary and turned to look back into the space. Drawing a deep breath in through my nose, I could smell a hundred years of incense lingering there. For a moment, just a fraction of a second, I felt…really good. Then all the fear of my current life came flooding back. But that split second of solace gave me the strength to go on.

AMOR VINCIT OMNIA

I made the sign of the cross and walked out of the church.

Fast steps, just a block to go. I'm a man on a mission and I'm determined to start it. I don't have any idea what I will face in there. The book's on the third floor, in an area reserved only for staff. Without even knowing why this book was so important, I should expect someone else may be trying to get this thing as well. And if I know about them, they may know about me.

I reach the front of the library. Pulling on the main door, I was surprised to find it fight against me with its sheer weight. I enter the lobby. Now, I love libraries. And I love old buildings. And the antiquarian in me is especially partial to marble anything. This lobby is a piece of art that deserves to be set up in a museum and admired by a million people a year. Instead, multi-colored marble insets in the tall walls and proud red marble columns stand unappreciated in a building that probably greets only a few hundred people a year. All that said, in that moment I sure was hoping that the internal security of this library was less impressive than the architecture and décor.

I opened the next set of doors and entered the building proper. I saw a tall frosted glass door on my left and another straight ahead. To my right I spied a guard in a light blue shirt behind a desk and...a square frame over the entrance to the library itself.

Was that one of those book detectors, you know, a machine to read the magnetized strips and prevent theft?

Or was it a metal detector?

Since I had a gun hidden at my belt, this mattered an awful lot. It didn't look like a metal detector. I had to make a decision. I could go ditch my gun and come back. Or I could go forward. There was virtually no security here. There's a single guard, who was reading a newspaper like he has never faced a crisis at this station before. I mean, if I step into that thing and it's a metal detector that screams out an emergency, what's he really going to do? In that case, I could at least bolt out of here. But that would also mean not fulfilling my mission.

Decision time, Andrew. That can't be a metal detector. That's a magnetic detector for books. This is, after all, a library.

I took out my little blue library pass and opened it. Walking toward the detector, I raised it to the guard, who looked at it briefly and returned to his newspaper. My heart skipped a beat as I stepped under the frame.

Nothing happened. I continued forward, down a bright hall, and entered a dark room. Doors were set almost randomly around me. Inside them, I assumed that functionaries went about the business of running a library, ignorant that at least one intelligence officer of a foreign government had just penetrated the place. To my left was an elevator and a set of stairs leading upward. Somewhere on the third floor, according to my briefer, was the book I was supposed to steal.

I was in.

I started up the stairs.

Chapter Five

Wednesday, March 16: 9:15 AM

I started up the stairs and felt a curious inconsistency beneath my feet. Looking more carefully at the steps, I saw that the marble was worn down from a century of traffic. The center was at least an inch lower than the sides. After just ten steps, I arrived at a platform to turn and start up another ten. I decided to walk as if I knew where I was going until I reached the top level. Then, from a strategically advantageous higher ground, I would explore downward and toward my target.

My ascent turned so fast that it felt like a spiral staircase. Finally I was at the top level of the library. The smell of old books hung in the air like an intellectual perfume. I love libraries. During my time in grad school, I used to go to the research library and just browse for hours in the stacks of old books there. Don't get me wrong. I'm a modern man who knows that the future is for all information to be digitized. I love the fact that I can now find out key information in mere seconds in an online search where before I had to thumb through paper books hoping that they held the answer.

But all that said, there was a charm to the days when the collective knowledge of humanity lay solemnly organized in rows of individually bound collections, printed on paper, bound in the old days with leather. And what this really accomplished was that after some years there was always a certain aroma of slightly moldering organic matter to old books. But that distinctive smell, for those of us who searched through the pages of time there, became linked with the additional feeling of exhilaration in the discovery of knowledge. It's kind of like how the smell of incense and burning candles makes you feel the presence of God when you enter a church.

I was at the top floor. Now, if you're an American, you're used to going into the stacks of books yourself and finding what you need. You learned how to use the calling cards, the Dewey Decimal System (and if you're under 25 years old you have no idea what I'm talking about). But in this library here in Bucharest, the *Hoi Polloi* are not trusted to go and find the books. Instead, you have to register yourself at a specific desk in one of several large reading halls distributed throughout the building. From your seat, you fill out a book request, writing down all the information on the volume, and then you give it to one of the "book runners." These highly trained individuals then go into the book stacks to get what you need and bring it to your seat. You may then read the books and take whatever notes you may, but you are not going to take that book out of that reading hall, let alone out of the library itself. In the clash of this archaic system and the modern world, I've seen young Romanians take pictures of every single page of a book with their phone, so they could get around the issue of not checking the thing out.

So that's what makes finding a book here a bit complicated. The book I'm supposed to steal is currently sitting in a cataloguing office. After it's catalogued, it gets put somewhere in the stacks. Both the cataloguing office and the stacks themselves are off-limits to the general public. And no books are allowed to leave the library. Removing the magnetic strip from a book is not actually enough, since it could still hold a residual charge. Even though I was able to sneak a Glock into this library, I was very nervous about trying to sneak this book out through that exit.

As I had told my briefer, the title seemed to describe a book that was 19th century. So let's imagine that this thing had waited in a collection of miscellaneous old books and no one knew a copy of it was sitting in Bucharest, Romania. Then, in the course of normal business, they finally get ready to catalog it, not knowing that this particular book is extraordinarily important to the premiere spy agency of the world's most powerful nation. Somehow that spy agency found out that the book was awaiting cataloguing here. They immediately move an agent into place to get this thing.

And the main reason for the urgency is that they are worried that someone else will be trying to get the thing as well.

So, the only explanation is that they think someone else has also possibly detected its presence through intercept. And they believe that that someone else wants the book just as badly as the NSA. And they've also presumably sent an agent to get the book. Jetting me over in an SR-71 was an attempt to put me into play at least as quickly as their agent.

I had to move fast. And my plan was now simple. The people running this library are not the intelligence experts that I could expect any moment to be making a play on this book. They are ordinary people who do not have the faintest idea how important this book is. And for that reason, they will not consider an intrusion as a massive security crisis.

I headed back down the stairs. One floor. Two floors. I arrived at the floor where the cataloguing office supposedly resides.

"Book Cataloguing," I read on a sign to the right of a door directly in front of me.

I took a deep breath. It was time to just make something happen. In I went.

AMOR VINCIT OMNIA

Bright florescent lights hung from the ceiling. A long table in the center of the room was covered with books. Two desks were set against the wall by the windows to the outside. I saw a coffee cup on one of them with the vapors of hot liquid still visible. So even though no one else was in the room, they were apparently not far away.

I scanned the books. They were different sizes, some obviously brand new. But on the far end of the table I spotted a pile of brown items that looked different—and old. I stepped silently toward them. Their titles were in a variety of European languages. In my focus, I deleted anything I saw that wasn't Latin.

And then I spotted it. *De Economia Orbis Terrarum.* It was a rather slim volume, bound in burgundy leather. The letters were embossed on the cover in gold leaf. In an instant I had picked it up and stuffed it between my back and my Glock.

"*Ce faceți aici?*" a voice said behind me.

Had this person seen me hide the volume? Only one way to find out.

"*Caut WC-ul,*" I said, putting no American accent in my Romanian. "*Unde este?*"

"*Acolo,*" he said, pointing out the door of the office. "*Mergeți la dreapta și după aceea la stânga.*"

He had obviously seen nothing. "*Mulțumesc,*" I said.

Now that I knew that the bathroom was to the right and then to the left, I decided that was as good a place as any to go right now. I pressed against the door thus marked and found myself in a room lit only by the sun pouring through a tall half-open window. I pushed it open the rest of the way and leaned out, taking a deep breath of fresh air. Outside I saw the roof of the building next door, just two stories below. So what should I do next?

A whistle.

I had just heard something. And it sounded like a whistle.

There, I heard it again.

Oh damn.

That's not a whistle.

That's a bullet fired through a silencer.

My Glock was drawn and pointed to the door of the bathroom. I was ready for anything. I was certainly ready to pull this trigger. I had unfortunately taken human lives in Iraq. I say 'unfortunately' only because in a perfect world there would be no killing. But in this imperfect world, I had served my country. But it had been at a distance, through a rifle. In Romania, during our escapade just a year ago, I had killed several more people with a Glock identical to the one I was holding.

"Aurora," I whispered.

AMOR VINCIT OMNIA

The door burst open. A man pointed a gun. I fired. Once, twice. I fired again. He crumbled. Outside in the hall, hurried footsteps moved this way.

There was only one escape. I hoisted myself through the window, dropping my gun in the process. Hanging from the sill, I let go. At the next story, I threw out my hands, grabbing at anything I could find. No luck, my hands slipped off the next window-sill and I was in free fall.

For a moment I was stunned. Oh, to sleep. No, I can't. Turning over, I saw the black tar roof of the neighboring building. No, this isn't right. They'll be...

Popcorn. That's what I heard. But that's what bullets sound like when they ricochet around you.

I bolted up and threw my pained body toward a shadow I hoped would shield me from attack.

The air struggled through my lungs. Muscles spasmed in my sides and I dropped to my knees.

I've got to get up. They're coming down here. I'm on the top of a roof. Find a way down.

I pushed myself to my feet and I shoot my gaze around. There's a ladder going down, but it's on the other side of the roof. Where's my gun?

I'm catching up to my senses. My gun is on the floor upstairs in that bathroom. I remember it now. And I'm under an outcrop of the building that hides me from the shooters in the window I jumped from. But they'll have a shot at me if I make for that ladder.

But if I don't move and one of them comes down, I'm done.

My only way to safety is to rush that ladder and try to get off this roof.

"Aurora," I again whisper. "It shouldn't end like this."

I'm running.

Popcorn again. There's the ladder. I dive and my hands find the top rung.

My body swings around and now I'm outside their range. Down I climb.

Two stories of this ladder and I drop onto a cobblestone street.

There are the sounds of sirens everywhere. Blue and red lights shine on the buildings as I drop to my knees and put my hands behind my head.

A car door slams.

High-pitched noises sailing above me mean that the enemy who sought my life are now gone.

"*Andrei?*" I hear. "*Ce faci aici?*"

I turn and look.

After all this time, just to gaze upon her face can still take my breath away. How is that fair?

"Aurora," I whispered.

Chapter Six

Wednesday, March 16: 10:00 AM

I sat at a massive mahogany table across from an official State portrait of Romanian President Traian Bascescu. His grin seemed to mock me, now in the custody of the SRI, Romania's premiere intelligence agency. But since the officer in charge at the scene was an acquaintance, I had not been subject to a search and still hid that book at my back.

All right, obviously she's more than an acquaintance. At one time, I was seriously in love with Aurora Zamfir. I probably still am. I probably always will be.

I heard a light tap at the door before it opened. Aurora entered alone.

"It's time for us to talk about what's going on," she said, sitting at the far end of the table from me. She was wearing a red dress suit, which I thought fabulously accented her blonde hair, currently worn in a long ponytail and cascading down her right shoulder.

"For starters, I know who you work for now. An investigator came all the way over here to find out what you had done for the SRI last year."

"I didn't do anything for the SRI," I said sharply. "I did that for my family!"

She rolled her eyes. "Andrew, do you remember the first time we met? You sound just like you did that night."

"Alright, let's start over. You know who I work for."

She spread open a manila folder. "No record of your legal entrance into Romania. I'm assuming you have a passport on you, though."

I took it out of my front pocket and slid it across the table to her.

Opening it, she pursed her lips in thought. "Look at you. The man who hated everything *Securitaté*. Stefan told me that you're really into this new job."

"You talk with Stefan?" I asked. "You mean even with this new promotion at the SRI you're allowed to associate with non-Romanian citizens?" My voice had carried a sarcasm that was ugly to me the moment the words left my mouth. But this had been the point over which she felt she had to break off our relationship.

"I can maintain casual contact," she said seriously. "I wish you and I could have done that."

A pain hit me in the chest and tears flooded my eyes. I looked up at her and saw that her eyes glistened back.

"I can't do that, Aurora."

"I know."

"Not yet," I said, adding a sincere smile.

She nodded and crossed her arms. "I still need to find out what's happening here."

"I'll tell you what I can," I said. "But you know that isn't much."

"So, like our last mission, I'm the one who has to give you all the information and see if you decide to help?"

"It worked well, right?"

"It did. We saved Romania together."

I chuckled, because those ridiculous words were more or less true.

"I'm going to tell you everything that led up to us taking down those men at the library. Our countries are strong allies. My official report already lists you as an NSA asset assisting us in our investigation. So I hereby grant you Top Secret clearance within the SRI."

"You had to get the director to do that last time. You have that authority all on your own now?"

She smirked. "Yes, Dr. Valquist. Now, one of those men, the one I'm assuming you shot in the bathroom before falling two stories out that window, had an irregularity on his passport."

"What nationality? When did he enter?"

"All three men had Swiss passports. But the date on the passport turned out to be off by a day from what the Swiss server reported back when the control officer swiped it."

"This was at Bucharest International Airport? When?"

"Very late last night. 11:30 arrival from Zurich. But when the control officer brought this up, he noticed the man got very nervous and seemed to look back at other people in his party for guidance."

"The control officer told the SRI all this?"

"He let the man through, but he told an SRI junior officer about the exchange. He said something seemed wrong. The man seemed nervous, even though there was no reason to not let him continue in."

"So how did you get involved?"

"Our officer at the airport called in a concern at 2 AM. He had found strangely little on the names of the three Swiss men in an Internet search. He felt that they seemed to carry names without a real past."

As she spoke, I found myself looking into her moving lips. They were gently accented with the faintest red lipstick. I remembered pressing mine against hers one night in this very building. Every fiber of my being had shouted in the joy of a love that we seemed to share. And every inch of my body surged with arousal to hold that celestial being again.

"And that's when I was called in," she said.

I realized I must have missed some points in between, but figured I could fake it from here.

"And you started following them this morning?"

"As I said, they were at the Lido Hotel..."

"I'm at the Intercontinental."

"NSA is rolling in it, huh?"

"They saw you were tailing them, that's why they tried to lose you?"

"Yes," she said. "They were on foot; we didn't know where they were going. Heading south, they scattered just as they reached the underground at *Piaţa Universităţii*."

"What time would this have been?" I asked.

"Just before Nine."

"Wow," I said. "You basically saved my life. I was just minutes ahead of them. If you hadn't slowed them down..."

"You wouldn't have succeeded in *your* mission at the library," she said. "And it's pretty obvious that they were there for the same thing. Any chance you're going to let me in on what that mission is?"

"So, you arrive at the library and then what?"

"We tapped into the surveillance videos of every important building around there and searched for them until we saw them entering the library, passes raised, with no problem."

"You rush over there and..."

"Just as we're coming to the library, I see a man jump out a window and I see two men start shooting down at him. We weren't in a strategic position to return fire, so I moved us over to the left, where I sensed we would have both cover and an angle to strike."

"Lesson Number One."

"Your Uncle taught me very well," she said, smiling. "Then, I see the man who jumped, dive off the roof, grab the ladder, and scramble down."

"And you take out the two in the window."

"I got one of them myself," she said. "That's something I learned on my own."

I hated the table that was so long that I couldn't reach out and take her hand right now. And I hated what had happened to the two of us.

"You're not going to tell me about your mission?" she asked.

"I can't."

She looked up at the ceiling. "I can say the word and you will be searched. What will we find if I do that?"

"Aurora…"

She looked at me calmly. "Andrew."

"Please don't."

She put her head in her hands and said nothing. A long silence hung between us, neither one of us wanting to break it. Because at least we were together.

"My heart shattered the day I broke us off," she said. "And I think about you every single day."

"There was no other way for us?" I asked, eyes again flooding with tears.

"There wasn't. No."

I reached back and pulled out the book. "This is why I was sent to the library," I said, putting it down on the table. "And I don't even know what it is myself."

She didn't even look at the book. She only looked into my eyes.

"I love you, Andrew Valquist. And I probably always will."

And that's when we both lost it.

I pushed myself away from the table and ran to her. She met me halfway. We were in a deep kiss, both of us sobbing, and then holding each other tightly. I released a year of pain, wondering about her, hating her for what she did, never able to stop loving her for everything she is.

"I miss you so much," she managed.

"I know," I whispered in her ear.

We slowly broke the embrace and held each other's shoulders.

"You have to go," she said.

"I do."

"You're in terrible danger."

"I am."

We both smiled again through tears.

"I'll pray for you," she said. "That's something you taught me."

"I need it," I said. "Listen, Aurora…"

She brushed her hand across my cheek. I searched for something more to say but found no words.

"Go now, Andrew," she said. "No one will stop you. God be with you."

I walked back and picked up my passport and the book. She had opened the door to the conference room.

"Go," she said softly, looking at the floor.

I walked out the door quickly.

Chapter Seven

Wednesday, March 16: 12:30 PM

I was tired. And pouring three glasses of red wine on top of this tiredness was probably not a great idea. But I had to do it. Seeing Aurora again was a trauma to my soul deeper than anything I had faced in that library this morning. I knew again with perfect clarity why I had fallen in love with her in the first place. And now I was painfully aware that after a year not a thing had changed.

"*Chelner*," I called out. "*Sunt gata să comand.*"

The waiter came over. I love how Romanian service personnel never write anything down. They memorize it on the spot. Or at least they try. And they frequently make mistakes.

"*Aş vrea o porţie de Calamari, vă rog,*" I said, handing him the menu.

He nodded and looked at the nearly empty carafe of wine on the table. I think for my own good he left without asking if I wanted a replacement.

Now, you may remember, I was supposed to work my way toward the Lipscani neighborhood so someone could take the book from me. They told me they would be able to find me. I still had that phone with me. And they must have seen I spent an hour at SRI headquarters after I left the library. But after everything that had happened, finding that gun and not knowing if I should take it (as it turned out I'd be dead without it), and then seeing Aurora, I was just not feeling all that obedient. They can find me if they want to. So I was relaxing in the outside seating area of my favorite seafood restaurants, just across the street from the Intercontinental.

Down the sidewalk, I spotted Hollings, the man from my limousine ride the previous day. He had apparently come on another flight, just in time to reap the rewards of my mission.

"May I join you?" he asked, approaching my table.

"Of course." I caught the eye of my waiter and lifted the carafe. He nodded as if unhappy. "But tell me your first name," I said.

"Dr. Valquist, you think you give the orders around here?" he asked hotly.

"I do!" I said. "Because you know from my file that, Doctor or no, I'm a dangerous man if I want to be."

"You need to calm down. My name's Dave. Do you have the book?"

"Yes, Dave. And call me Andrew." I said, and then drained the last of the wine.

"And what about this time at SRI?"

"They were following the other interested party. I got away without their help. But I had no choice but to go with them after that."

"Understood. They sent a cable to the NSA informing us that they had accidentally detained one of our agents and then released him."

"That sounds about right."

The waiter arrived with my Calamari and the carafe.

"*Mulțumesc frumos*," I said, watching him fill two glasses.

He bowed slightly and left without a word.

I took a deep sip off my glass. "Now talk to me about the gun."

"You deserve an explanation," Dave said. "We had placed it in the luggage in case we wanted you to enter the library armed. But we decided to send you in without it. And that's why I didn't say anything."

"You assumed I wouldn't go through those bags?"

"Actually, yes."

"That's not implausible." I picked up my fork but then set it down, opting to just eat the meal with my fingers.

"Oh my God, that's good!" I said. "Feel free to eat up. We can always order more."

He shook his head. "That's okay. But I will have that drink." He raised his glass. "Congratulations, Dr.

Valquist—Andrew. You've successfully completed your first mission."

"It's a success when your agent doesn't go where you tell him to and then borders on the insubordinate?"

Dave laughed. "I've seen it all. The better they are, the more, well, willful they become."

I reached behind and extracted the book. "Here's what this was all about," I said, dropping it in front of him.

"You might as well put it back," he said.

"Why?"

"I don't know any Latin. You're still the subject matter expert."

I finished the Calamari, drained my glass, and refilled it. "I'm doing nothing until I know everything you know about this case."

"You're not cleared for it."

"Then clear me and get talking."

"You really think you're something, don't you?"

"Trained as a commando before the end of high school, expert in multiple languages, Iraq War veteran, yeah, you don't have twenty more agents just like me. So I'm done taking these orders blindly."

"I guess we have no choice," he said. "Those people that tried to kill you today already have a copy of that book."

I thought that through. "Then they want to keep anyone else from seeing it."

"And that's because they are in the final stages of a plan to destroy civilized society as we know it. And that book is their blueprint."

I took another deep sip off my glass and, putting it on the table, realized I should slow down. I needed at least a few wits about me to follow this story.

"How do we know all those things?"

"I'm the director of a special division at the NSA that tracks dozens of shadowy extra-national organizations. We piece together everything we can from historical record and, of course intercept."

"Then you must have known about SABIA, the group my twin and I helped take down here in Romania last year?"

"Absolutely. But since they were only targeting Romania, we didn't get involved. You did nice work, though."

"Thanks. What's the history behind this book?"

"Have you ever heard of Frederic Adler?"

"No."

"Not surprising. No one has," he said. "He was a philosopher of sorts in Zurich in the early 1800's. He wrote a treatise on economics. There are only two copies in existence."

"Concerning the Economy of the World?" I asked. "The world was hardly a unified economy back then."

"He was a visionary. He described a gradual process in which the various nations became economically intertwined. He even included unlikely areas such as the Arab world and the Far East in his futuristic thinking. And then, in a final chapter, he described how one could destroy that world economy. We know all about this book, but we've never before actually seen the thing."

"Who are the people with the other copy?" I asked.

"The Emperor in Vienna was afraid of this book," he said. "He sent agents who bought up every copy they could find and destroyed them. He kept one copy for himself. But, based on the printing numbers, there was one volume unaccounted for. It was purchased by a man who then disappeared into Hungary."

"That would be the one I found this morning at the library."

"Yes. It somehow was sitting in a pile of old and uncatalogued books. When we saw a mention of it in electronic intercept, we went into action. We knew that if we didn't..."

"The other group would get it and destroy it so no one would be able to guess their future moves. But who is this group? And how did they end up with the Emperor's copy?"

"From what we can piece together, one of the emperor's own advisers was an admirer of Adler and stole it to study the man's thought in depth. We don't even know the man's name, but he founded a secret society that believes the only way to honor their hero is to prove his theories correct."

"By destroying the world economy as Adler described in the last chapter."

"Exactly."

I knew what I needed to know…and headed back into my wine. "So it doesn't even matter if Adler was right, the fact that these people believe him means they will do what he said. And that…"

"Is in that book," the man said.

"How big and powerful is this group?"

"No idea. But they seem to focus their efforts on placing agents in sensitive positions to gain an influence well beyond their numbers. And because of that we assumed they would have access to electronic intercept as good as our own."

"And you were right. That means they have a member inside an agency capable of such intercept. Forgive me, but since I didn't finish NSA orientation, who else could have done that?"

The man smiled. "Most any big country. Probably not Switzerland, though. If I had to guess, they have a member highly placed with French Intelligence."

"But their three agents came from Switzerland."

"SRI told you that?" Dave asked smiling. "Or more accurately, Aurora Zamfir?"

I chuckled. "I can see you've done your homework."

Dave nodded. "So the Adlerites seem to have a member in the Swiss foreign ministry. And that person made them fake passports."

"What's next, then?"

Dave refilled both our glasses. "Drink up, Andrew. And then go across the street and sleep this off. Later tonight you're on a flight back to Washington where you'll start your regular job. Your first assignment there will be to translate that book and see if you can figure out what they're planning to do."

I picked up my glass and touched it to my lips. My brain was swirling and I knew I'd had enough. I almost lost my lunch flying over here sober. I sure didn't want to attempt a supersonic flight buzzed. "If you'll excuse me, I need a nap."

"Be ready to leave at seven," he said.

"I'm on the SR-71 again?"

"No. Business Class from the airport."

I sat back down. "Well that changes everything, Dave. *Chelner! Mai aduceţi-ne o porţie de Calamari şi o carafă de vin!*"

Chapter Eight

Friday, March 18: 6:00 AM

It was my first day back to work after the incursion to Romania. The NSA had given me the previous day off to rest. I wouldn't have really needed it. My flight back had been a vacation all in itself. On business class, you can hear the magic words, "Would you like a refill of your champagne before we take off?" Even so, we got to Baltimore-Washington International Airport kind of late. So, I took the day when it was offered.

I had a piece of paper with my new office written on it. OPS2B 3012. I didn't even yet have all of my log-on information to do real work. I assumed that could come today.

My apartment was in Columbia, Maryland, just ten minutes west from Fort Meade, where the NSA was located. I get off Hwy 32 at the NSA exit, Canine Road, named after the first director of the organization. My agency badge is going to get me past the guard gate. I roll the window down and show the armed guard my credentials. He touches the badge, flips it over and gives it greater scrutiny than the guard up at the FANX had done. I guess they run a tighter ship at the Fort itself.

It's early and I had been told there would be spots available in the parking lot to the right of the road I entered on. I was in luck. To the left I saw a wasteland of empty parking that would be full by nine in the morning. This is indeed a huge facility.

I approached the main buildings. They are towering dark blue glass wonders. Up the front steps. Inside the lobby, I passed through a row of turnstiles, and moved along.

And then, I saw it. Stepping forward a few more feet down a darkened walkway, the wall at a T-Crossing of the hallways displayed the symbols of the NSA. There is the blue circle, with an eagle set atop it. The eagle holds a key, symbolic of a cryptological key. Next to it is the symbol of the CSS, the Central Security Service. The CSS is the technical name for the military elements who work at NSA. The symbol of the CSS is a blue circle with a star and the seals of the five military elements that contribute personnel: the Naval Network Warfare Command, Marine Corps, the Army Intelligence and Security Command, the Air Force Intelligence, Surveillance and Reconnaissance Agency, and the U.S. Coast Guard. People sometimes forget that the Coast Guard are a part of the military. Not only are they military, but they yearly suffer per capita casualties as bad as the other services. Rescuing boaters and fighting drug traffickers are inherently dangerous things.

I walk to the left at the T-Crossing and come around to a much brighter space. And there in front of me is a black marble triangle structure set against the wall. And as I approached it, I saw it was a memorial to all who had given their lives in the service of the NSA. A little more than a day earlier, I had faced gunfire for the agency. But here were the names of men and women who had made the ultimate sacrifice. I scanned the names. Lots of military, judging from the ranks. And then I saw something curious—"Identity Withheld." I wondered if I had been killed whether my name would have been withheld. I made the sign of the cross and prayed for the souls of all these honored dead. And I resolved that I would do so every day for as long as I walked down this hall.

I arrived at the elevator bank. There are eight—four on each side of a hall, past which I see a cafeteria. A collection of civilians and soldiers slowly assembled. I saw a Marine officer approach and had to suppress the automatic reaction to give him a salute. Isn't that funny? A year out of the service and I still think about these things.

OPS2B 3012, I reread on the slip of paper. I didn't think this building had thirty floors, so I assumed that this meant the third floor. The door opened. In we went. Now, I'm in good shape. And so I could have taken the stairs. But something about this first day, not to mention the adventure I had just completed, made me feel I deserved the elevator experience.

Someone else had pressed the third floor even before I entered. So I waited. Second floor. And then mine.

Several other people poured out with me. I was in no real hurry, so I didn't feel the urgency to ask for help in finding my room. As it was, there was ample wall signage to help me finally find my way.

The door was disarmingly light. And even though I had gone through multiple security checks, I was surprised that there wasn't some final DNA test before I could go into my office. I entered.

And it wasn't really an office. It was a sweep of cubicles. Miles to my right and endlessly fading to my left. I could have entered at the "office" number twenty doors down and just walked down this hallway through the cubicles and arrived at this spot. It would have made more sense to number the cubicles than the doors. Whatever. I'd seen things a thousand times more stupid in the Army. And this was, after all, an agency of the Department of Defense.

At this early hour just a few people were scattered at desks. Even though the whole door thing did not make any official sense, I had been sent to this door, so

I believed that my desk was somewhere closer to this spot than the other side of the building. I saw a kid sitting at a desk, typing away furiously at a computer. I describe him as a kid because he looked like he could have been sixteen, even though I knew he was probably a legal adult.

"Greetings, young man," I said. "I was told to report here this morning. Do you know who my boss might be?"

He looked up at me in a momentary confusion. Suddenly I saw terror in his eyes. "Dr. Valquist?"

I put out my hand to shake. "The very same."

He scrambled to his feet. "I'm so sorry, sir. Um, let me show you to your office."

"This cubicle next to you seems to be empty," I said, pulling out the chair. "I'd be grateful if you could just help me get logged on to my accounts."

The young man did not sit back down. "Sir, your office is not out here."

"Well then where is it?"

"Come with me, sir."

Since he was walking away, I pretty much had to follow him. He led me through a maze of cubicles until we arrived at an actual door.

"Right through here, sir."

I stepped in and saw a simple room, with a gray desk set against the wall. A computer console sat atop it. It was otherwise no different from the work stations outside, apart from being surrounded by four walls.

"Why do I get this place?" I asked. "I'm the new hire. When does our boss get here?"

He smiled in bewilderment. "You don't know? Dr. Valquist, you're the boss."

I leaned against the doorway. "What's your name?"

"Matt."

"Where do we keep the coffee, Matt?"

"I'll get you a cup, sir."

No, Matt. That's not how we do things."

***

It was now late in the morning. A techie had come by this little office and given me my log-on information. A phone call from Dave had explained that I had been put in charge of a special group assembled to continue the mission I started in Bucharest. My "Tiger Team," as it's apparently called, were now all at their desks. And I was their boss. The Tiger Team's job was to translate the book I stole from the library as quickly as possible and also try to figure out what this shadowy group would do next.

It was time to meet and greet my team.

As I stepped out of my walled office, the three workers were hunched over their keyboards. I had only met Matt, but I had briefed myself on all of them from their resumes in my email.

Matt was just twenty years old. He had started at the NSA as a high school intern. He didn't even go to college and got a job at the agency as a secretary. He trained into intelligence reporting two years later. He was on the team because he had four years of high school Latin. By my own experience, I knew that meant he was virtually worthless as a Latin translator.

Next to him was Norman. African-American. Marine. He had been in Afghanistan in the invasion phase. But he also had solid Latin credentials. He had graduated from the Latin School of Chicago, an academy where students start that language in elementary grades and continue through high school.

To his left sat Christine. Her bright red hair almost blinded me as I looked over the group. She was the true linguist of the team. She had her Bachelor's and Master's degrees in Classical Studies. The agency hired her merely for her language learning abilities and immediately put her into intensive Arabic study. A year later, they have plucked her out of that and put her at a desk here and she doesn't even know why.

Finally, there was Tori. An Army girl. No Latin whatsoever, but she was an expert at researching data through the classified and open source systems. I should define "open source" for you. That means everything available in the real world. For practical purposes, that means mastery over the internet.

"Hello," I said, stepping toward them. "I'm Andrew Valquist."

Tori and Norman jumped from their seats and stood at attention. Matt and Christine turned and stood more slowly, with no disrespect intended.

"At ease," I said, in military protocol. "I know all about you. I've read your files. And I'm impressed with each and every one of you."

They looked back at me like deer in the headlights. I didn't like the dynamic.

"My name is Andrew. And we are all on a first name basis here. Is that understood?"

An awkward silence.

"Tori, what's my name?" I said.

"Andrew, sir."

"Just Andrew, okay?"

She laughed. "Yes, Andrew."

"We have a funny little job. It's in Latin. And I'm sure none of you thought that Latin mattered anymore in this day and age. We need to translate a book. It's not very big. But it's not terribly small either. And we need to do this fast."

"Just give me my orders, sir," Norman said.

I put my hand on his shoulder. "Norman, my name is Andrew."

He winced, clearly uncomfortable with the informality I was requesting. "Andrew. Put me to work. Our computer dictionary has Latin, not that I really need it."

"Permission to speak," Christine said.

"Of course."

"I wasn't hired at the NSA for my Latin knowledge," she said. "I was hired because I know how to learn languages. And I'm not happy about being pulled out of my Arabic studies. I am officially requesting a return to my previous assignment."

I nodded to her. "*ana 'afham,*" I said. "*laakin ana bi-Haaja 'ilayki.*" I hoped she would appreciate being told she was needed on the team.

"Your Arabic is good," she said.

"*Shukran.*"

"Far better than mine," she said, looking at the floor.

"I need you on this team," I said. "I was hired as an Arabic linguist as well. We'll advance your Arabic skills here, don't worry."

"So where do I fit in?" Matt asked.

"You're my chief reporter," I said. "But be ready to learn other things."

I knew from my email that I was slated to spend the rest of the day in some rapid orientation procedures. I set the team to some research on various points. I managed to return to them at 1500, 3 PM, that is. I stood in our work spaces looking them over. My Tiger Team. We should really get some serious work done on that book yet today. But I decided that the team needed to connect first, to be truly effective.

"Matt, where do people go to get great Mexican food around here?"

"I really like La Fiesta up at Arundel Mills."

"I'm buying. Let's go."

***

As we ate some spectacular Mexican food and drank beers, I listened to the members of my team tell tales of where they came from.

Matt was actually from Jessup, just one exit south from the Fort. He had spent his life seeing those massive buildings and getting a job there was a dream come true. He was just so uncertain what he had to offer to the group. Everyone assured him that he was a valued member of the team.

Norman was from the south side of Chicago but had gotten a scholarship to go to the Latin School. His teachers were terribly disappointed in him when he turned down competing bids from several Ivy League schools to join the Marines, something he felt duty-bound to do for reasons he was quiet about.

Tori was from Fargo, North Dakota. She had joined the Army because it seemed the only career path for a mediocre high school student. But the Army intelligence tests identified that an extraordinarily gifted young person had apparently just fallen through the cracks. She had become a distinguished intelligence analyst in the Counterterrorism Office, only to be sent to my team.

Christine was distant at first, not aloof, just uncomfortable. But as she told us about the pride she felt when she got her acceptance letter from the NSA, I saw her warm to her colleagues. We learned that this DC native was the daughter of a one-time Senator, a Georgetown graduate, and a reality TV junkie.

When my turn to share came around, I told them about my twin brother, Stefan, an Orthodox priest and the fact that we are so close that we speak together every single day. I didn't tell them about a mother who raised us as anti-communist commandos in order to liberate Romania, a plan that she didn't live to carry out. I mentioned my Army service and time in Iraq. And I told them how proud I was to serve beside them. They didn't know it, but I was about to announce that we would work weekends and overtime until that book was completed. But for now, we were going to relax and celebrate. None of us knew, as we laughed and smiled in the orange glow of candlelight, that the next week would test us sorely and that human civilization depended on our efforts.

Chapter Nine

Saturday, March 19: 10:00 AM

It's Saturday morning and I've ordered my team to work. They didn't grumble last night about it at all. They know we have so much to do that we can't just take two days off and start on Monday morning as if the world isn't in peril on weekends. And, you'll be relieved to know, the NSA is not really closed on Saturday and Sunday. Anyone driving by could tell that most people who work there have a normal Monday through Friday schedule. But every important team I met in the offices nearby ours had personnel there on the weekend to process and assess the intelligence that continued to come in.

Now, I want to apologize to you, dear reader, that I am going to be speaking around some intelligence matters at times. Even in that previous paragraph, notice that the phrase "process and assess" intelligence that "comes in" is intentionally vague. How does this intelligence "come in"? Well, that's really the meat and potatoes of what it means for something to be Top Secret. It is common knowledge and even unclassified that the National Security Agency obtains intelligence through the interception of communications signals. Even so, there are just details about that which I am not legally allowed to share. Truth be told, since I'm a linguist, there's very little about the technical matters that I even understand.

I had given everyone a job. Matt was typing the Latin text out and sending it to Norman and Christine to begin translating. We tried to scan it in but the font returned so many typos that we abandoned that method. Tori was put on the task of assembling a description of everything known about this group that had the other copy of the book. I was taking everything Norman and Christine translated and then giving it what we call a "QC." QC stands for Quality Control. The principle at the NSA is that everything that is translated, even if translated by a Ph.D. expert in her field, must be looked at by another linguist who has the certifications to perform the "Quality Control." And that's because anyone can make a mistake. And since this stuff really matters, we had better not issue a report that contains a simple error. Now, later in that day I would be the prime mover in issuing a report that was, in retrospect, wrong. But it was not an error in linguistic knowledge. It was an error in interpretation. But we'll get to that later.

You only get assigned the status of a "QCer" after you have passed the Agency's language certification tests and proven that you have a high level in the language. But there is no formal Latin language certification at the NSA, for the obvious reason that no one speaks it. So, in the case of my team, I made the executive decision that I would be the QCer for Norman and Christine.

As they sent me their translations, I would look over what they did, comparing it to the Latin text Matt had typed. Christine was very good. I made just a few corrections here and there. For instance, I thought the translation of a present active participle would be clearer if you broke it out into a full verb. But then I examined Norman's work. In the very first sentence I looked at, I realized that I was not sure what the original text even meant. Norman had produced a translation that was clear and straightforward. I brought up the computer dictionary Norman had shown me how to use. It contains dictionaries to the most obscure dialects in the world. And, *Gratias Deo*, it contained Latin as well. Anyway, I studied the passage and reached two conclusions. First, Norman's translation was spot-on. Second, I could not have correctly translated this passage. In other words, Norman was better at Latin than I was. Far better.

I walked over to the team. "We're going to be changing up the duties a little bit. Matt, you'll be sending the typed pieces to me and Christine. Christine, you and I will be the lead translators and we'll be sending our work to Norman for QC."

"Sir!" Norman said, standing from his seat. "Why? What did I do wrong?"

"Norman! You didn't do anything wrong. You're just better than me! I need the best Latin expert on this team to be the QCer. And that's you."

"How did you get so good?" Christine asked him, smiling.

"I've been doing Latin since Second Grade," he said.

"We're going to learn a lot from him," I said. "Let's get back to work."

As I said earlier, the NSA never shuts down. And that means the cafeteria, even in the middle of the night, is staffed by a short order cook who can at least whip you up a burger and fries. The people in the cafeteria are uncleared, meaning they do not have a security clearance and there are red lines on the floor that tell them the point past which they may not cross. And there are also signs everywhere reminding agents that they are in a non-classified area and must not engage in talk that is classified. So, for lunch on that Saturday, I treated myself to a burger and fries cooked by an uncleared worker. As I write this, I'm uncleared myself, and indeed, I spent most of my life uncleared. So I always treated them with the dignity that they deserve as human beings. And when you consider that an uncleared employee, working a Midnight shift at the NSA, contributes in a meaningful way to the morale of

AMOR VINCIT OMNIA

people working critical missions, we should recognize these people as patriots whose service keeps our nation safe.

I got back from lunch to find a tall brunette waiting at my office door. Her light blue and frilly dress seemed a bit formal for a Saturday at the NSA, but I certainly wasn't going to complain to her supervisor.

"Hello?" I asked.

"Dr. Valquist, nice to meet you," she said, grabbing my hand and shaking it. "I'm the Team Chief from the shop down the hall. Our Arabic linguists are all busy with an especially pressing matter. And someone said you knew Arabic. So, could you look at something for me?"

"*I'm looking at something right now.*" (Hey, I thought it, sure, but I didn't say it out loud!)

"Of course," I replied.

So, here's the issue. She brought me this "piece" because in it, someone had communicated something she thought was potentially worrisome.

And I already knew from my experience in Iraq that a particular word in the "piece" was a known cover-term for an attack.

Maybe you're not familiar with the concept of a "cover-term." Let's imagine you and I want to talk on the phone and plan a surprise birthday party for your spouse. But we worry that she may overhear us.

So, to keep our little surprise party a secret, you and I come up with a "cover-term" in advance. So, every time I say, "Hey, let's talk about our upcoming 'fishing trip'," it's really a conversation about the surprise party.

"So, have you made any arrangements for the 'fishing trip'," I ask.

"Yeah, I've already scoped out the 'fishing spot'."

Except "fishing spot" means "restaurant" by another pre-arranged cover-term.

So, the piece contained a well-known, even openly published, cover-term for "attack."

I translated the piece in my head. It wasn't at all difficult. But the process did require a second set of eyes/ears. "Christine," I said. "I'd like you to do a QC on a piece."

Christine confirmed that my literal translation was accurate.

"So what do you want to do next?" I asked Beth, as her name turned out to be.

"I don't know," she said. "Do you think this should be reported?"

Now, I haven't yet explained the whole "reporting" process. The NSA takes intercepted communications and turns them into intelligence reports. These reports go via the classified network to various intelligence consumers. If it's terrorism related, for instance, you can imagine that the White House is an automatic recipient of the report.

So Beth wanted to know whether this "piece" should be turned into a report. Now, I can tell you, having been in a war zone, I want to know if there is even a hint of a possibility of a rumor of danger out there before I step outside my door. So, for me, this was a no-brainer. Of course we issue a report. And that report will contain the necessary caveats. We'll explain in the report that this "word," while it is a well-known cover-term, may be literally true. In other words, sometimes a cigar is just a cigar.

Based on my opinion, we issued this report. I insisted on this because I imagined that people would want to know about even the hint of a possibility of a rumor of an attack.

And it turned out that, in this case, a cigar was just a cigar.

***

My team worked again on Sunday. Now, as you've been able to deduce from previous parts of the story, I'm a Church-goer. And I wasn't going to make my team work at the expense of attending whatever service their tradition held. And I brought this up on Saturday afternoon. Norman, it turned out, was a Catholic who would be attending Mass on Saturday evening. So he would then be at his desk on Sunday morning to continue QC'ing. Tori was a practicing Lutheran who said she would go to the early service at her church on Sunday and come in right after that. Matt and Christine were non-religious and would be at work first thing in the morning.

And that brings us to me. The Eastern Orthodox Sunday Liturgy is ordinarily two hours. Since I was requiring eight hours from my team, I felt bad about being away for so long. So I set my alarm for 3:00 AM, went in to the NSA and translated enough material to keep Norman busy QC'ing for several hours, and then went to a Liturgy in nearby Columbia that started at 9:30. I was back with the team by noon. And we spent the rest of the day hard at work translating that book. We were making excellent progress. We turned off our computers late that Sunday afternoon, well ahead of schedule. And I didn't know then that I made a horrible error the previous day.

Chapter Ten

Monday, March 21: 7:00 AM

I had just opened my email, when I heard a knock at my door.

"Dr. Valquist?"

I turned to see Dave. "So you work in this building too?" I asked.

"No," he said. "But I've been called in here to tell you something important."

I turned from the computer screen. "This doesn't sound good."

"You've been summoned to attend the Director's morning briefing at Nine. They expect you to explain that report that went out."

I knew immediately what report he was talking about. And I felt my blood pressure surge thirty degrees. "What's going on?"

"One of our embassies shut down because of that report. They worried that they might be the target."

"So?" I asked. "Maybe that was a good idea."

"The Intelligence forces investigated the matter. And it turns out…"

A cigar was just a cigar.

I sat there numb and thought through the piece. I heard Dave almost screaming at me. Our Ambassador was pissed. The RSO (Regional Security Officer at the Embassy) was even calling the report "reckless." The CIA was saying the report was unnecessarily "sensationalist."

And now I had to explain to the Director himself why I sent out that report.

Knowing now that "a cigar was just a cigar," the piece suddenly did seem mundane. And now, in light of this information, it seemed obvious to me that the piece had not been talking about an attack, but was talking only about a real cigar.

But obviously hindsight is 20/20.

I seemed to be in trouble. All I could do was explain why I did what I did.

***

I sat at a large table in a room that seemed slightly too small for the furniture. The walls were covered with historical scenes and also maps of regions in Afghanistan and Iraq that were quite current in their importance. Other people entered slowly and took seats. They greeted one another with a relaxation that told me they weren't there to explain their rash actions to a man who reported directly to the President. Most were military officers, and high ranks at that. A few others were well dressed civilians who looked to be about fourteen places up the management chain from me. I had not expected to be summoned to a meeting with the Director of the NSA that day and so I was dressed in my normal white dress shirt and khaki slacks. I wished I at least had a tie to throw on. But no such luck.

Everyone stood and so, I did as well. In walked the Director of the National Security Agency. Now, this Four Star General would eventually leave the NSA and just a little later become the Director of the CIA. He's enjoying a well-deserved retirement now after over four decades of distinguished service to our nation. But that morning, he had called me on the carpet to explain why the CIA and State Department were crying foul over the report I sent out.

He told everyone to take their seats and I found myself listening to his regular morning briefing. This Colonel gave a report about optimizing resources, followed by that Suit talking about leveraging assets. I was starting to wonder if I was really supposed to be there at all. Finally, the Director puts his finger on the agenda in front of him.

"Alright, last order of business," he says, and turns to me. "You must be Dr. Valquist. I'd like you to please explain everything that went into your decision to send out that report which has the rest of the Intelligence Community so mad at me this morning."

The disapproving eyes of an entire room tore into me like laser beams.

Here I was, on my eighth day of employment at the NSA. I had already been to Eastern Europe on a super-sensitive clandestine mission for the agency. Then I had been put in charge of a Tiger Team. And now I had put out a controversial report that results in me sitting in front of the Director himself to explain myself. My career at the NSA was either off to an excellent or a horrible start.

As calmly as I could, I explained that the piece included a clear use of a known cover-term. I also pointed out that the final report we issued did remind readers that there was no way to know for certain if this was a cover-term or an innocent event. I closed by stating that my experiences under fire in Iraq had left me quite unwilling to just sit on something that might be important. I would always err on the side of caution and put the information out in case someone else had a different piece of the puzzle.

The Director had sat and listened to me carefully. "And if you had this to do over again?"

"General," I said. "I issued that report based on the information I had at the time. And I would do it all over again, even if it means I lose my job."

He smiled. "That's good enough for me. I'll push back and tell the other agencies that the NSA stands by its report. Just because it's proven wrong doesn't mean it wasn't the right thing to do at the time."

I felt as if a ton of bricks were lifted from my shoulders.

"And you're also the one who got us that book?"

"Yes, sir," I said.

"How's it coming?"

"We're translating it and we hope to soon figure out what that group is planning."

"I make only one request of you," he said.

"Yes?"

"What you're doing is too important to be taking even a minute out of your time to work for another team."

I realized he was right. "Yes, sir. I understand."

As he stood, I rose from my seat quickly.

"I'm glad you're here, Dr. Valquist," he said, shaking my hand. "There are yet greater things in store for you."

As I rode the elevator back down to earth, his final words haunted me. They seemed to imply something even beyond the current Latin project.

***

I was getting ready to call it a day when I heard a knock at the door. A finely suited man stepped inside. I recognized him from the meeting earlier.

"The Director asked me to deliver something to you," he said, stretching out his hand.

I took from him a small bronze coin and I knew from a glance what I was holding. "Presented by the Director" was engraved around one side. This was a cherished memento of my briefing to the very head of the NSA. Higher officers give their subordinates coins in recognition of various achievements. In military circles, when a group of people gather for a celebration, frequently each person presents the highest ranked coin they hold. The holder of the lowest ranked coin has to pay for the drinks. The Director of the NSA is a Four Star General. It was unlikely that I would ever have to buy another drink in a military gathering.

Chapter Eleven

Thursday, March 24: 1:30 PM

The team sat around a large table in one of the conference rooms in OPS2B. Copies of our completed work, Latin text and English translation on facing pages, were strewn about. Tired smiles abounded.

"I want to thank everyone for a job well done," I said. "We got this thing translated days faster than I thought possible."

"Not a minute too soon," Matt added. "I'm typing Latin out in my dreams."

"And so it's time to put the pieces together," I continued. "Tori, let's hear your background report."

She opened a manila folder on the table. "I've got a more detailed package ready to email you all," she said. "But here it is in a nutshell. Our Branch knows little more about this group than what we've inherited from our counterparts at MI-5. A small number of well-placed people who are devoted to the teachings of Frederic Adler intend to destroy the world economy with some devastating attack at a spot Adler indicates in the final chapter of the book."

"I have a question," Christine said.

"Yes?"

"Why would Adler even want to describe an attack that could destroy the world economy?"

"Well, partly as an intellectual exercise," she said. "But he also took on anarchist views later in life. He seemed to believe that this would further those goals."

"Why didn't we start with the final chapter when we translated?" Matt asked. "If that's the only one that matters to us."

I smiled. "My boss Dave wanted the whole thing done so we didn't risk missing any potential clues. There doesn't seem to be any urgency about the timing of this devastating attack."

"Makes sense," he said. "I guess."

"So, that said, we've all now read the whole thing. Including the last chapter. Any ideas?"

"The last chapter is just a series of quotes and maxims," Norman said. "If this thing is pointing at a location, it's somehow encoded."

"What about an acrostic?" Tori said.

"What's an acrostic?" Matt asked.

"First letters of words or sentences forming a message," Christine said. "Are they even done in Latin?"

"Absolutely," I said. "And Frederic Adler would know the concept," I added, opening my copy and thumbing to the end. The others did likewise.

AMOR VINCIT OMNIA

"I was concentrating so hard on the meaning of the Latin that I wouldn't have seen it," Norman said.

"**S**ic transit gloria mundi," I read from the first line. "Thus passes the glory of the world."

"**E**rrare est humanum," Christine continued. "To err is human."

"**R**epetitio est mater studiorum," Norman added. "Repetition is the mother of learning."

"**O**mnia vincit amor," I read. "Love conquers all things."

"The original quote from Vergil's *Eclogues* reads *Amor vincit omnia*," Norman said. "This *was* reordered to produce an acrostic."

All of us scanned downward. A few more lines and I let out an audible gasp.

"What is it?" Tori asked.

"You've done it!" I wrote out the resulting message and started reading it to the group. "*Sero te amor*."

"And what does it mean?" Tori asked.

"*Sero te*..." Norman said. "St. Augustine, right?"

"God, you're good. *Sero te amavi*," I said. "Late have I loved thee. It's a well-known line from St. Augustine's *Confessions*."

"But '*amor*' is a noun," he said. "Late thee Love? That's not grammatical."

"But it's obviously intended to be an allusion to St. Augustine, you agree."

"Undoubtedly."

"*Ad nuces*," I continued. "To nuts."

"To nuts?" Matt said. "You mean like 'From soup to nuts'?"

"No," Norman replied. "There's another Latin maxim for that. *Ab ovo usque ad mala*. From egg to apples."

"And that's the quote that gives us the '*A*' of '*ad nuces*'," Christine said. "That can't be a coincidence."

"No," Norman said. "There are a lot of layers of meaning here. Now, there's a saying '*Redire ad nuces*', meaning 'To return to nuts', that is, 'To return to one's childish ways'."

"Honestly, Norman," Christine said. "How do you know all these things?"

"I've been memorizing Latin quotes since I was seven," he said, smiling at her.

"*Nisi barca stet salua*," I said, finishing the message. "Unless...*barca*?...stands safe?" It wasn't a question, I was just very confused by the final section.

"What's *barca*?" Christine asked, curling puzzled eyebrows at the passage.

"A reference to Hamilcar Barca?" Tori asked. "That's Hannibal's father."

"And like St. Augustine, from North Africa," I said.

"Wouldn't *barca* be cognate to *Mubarak*?" Christine asked.

"Yes," Norman said. "It would mean *blessed* in a number of Semitic languages."

Christine smiled broadly at him. "And you know this because, why?"

"I dabble in a lot of things," he said.

"We're definitely getting close here," I said. "And the adjective *salua*, safe, is feminine, like *barca*."

"So it's referring to a woman," Tori asked. "I forget. Was Augustine married?"

"No," I said slowly, thinking through the issues. "But his mother Monica was important to his conversion."

"So..." Matt continued. "Unless she stood safe, her son would have returned to his childish ways?"

"Not bad," I said. "*Barca* is also a Medieval Latin word for ship."

"Isn't the Church called the Barque of St. Peter?" Norman asked. "The Church as a ship with St. Peter as the Captain?"

"That's the final piece of the puzzle," I said. "Adler is making a play on words here. *Barca* is three different things. It's a Semitic feminine adjective for 'blessed'. And Adler would have known that. It's also a word that reminds us of someone from North Africa. And it's a word for Church. And Adler would have known all that too. And we know beyond a doubt that the whole thing is connected to St. Augustine. So, putting it all together, the *blessed* woman Monica, from North Africa, and a Church. Does anyone happen to know where St. Monica is buried?"

"Where?" Matt asked excitedly.

"I don't know myself," I said.

"I've got this," Tori said, walking across the room. She logged on to a work station computer by the conference room door. Just a moment later she turned around slowly.

"St. Monica is buried in a Church dedicated to her son. And it's in Rome."

We sat in silence a moment, absorbing the information.

"In retrospect," I started, "Rome makes a lot of sense. The economic impact of a disruption to the Church would itself be devastating. But even as a European capital, Rome is fully interconnected."

"But so what?" Christine said. "It doesn't take a rocket scientist to guess that destroying Rome would cripple the world economy."

"You could probably cripple the world's economy by destroying any European capital," I said. "But our mission is to stop this crazy group from doing it in that particular place just because they want to vindicate Adler's theory. And that means knowing where they think they need to attack."

"So, now that we've solved the puzzle, this attack will be stopped?" Matt asked.

"We can assume that the group had solved this puzzle long ago with their own copy of the book," Tori said. "But in the modern world they have been waiting to acquire a weapon capable of destroying an entire city."

"A nuclear weapon?" he said. "That's quite a long shot for this little group."

"Makes sense, though," Christine added. "Adler was ahead of his time. He knew that eventually warfare would develop something big enough to do it."

"Now that we know where they think they're supposed to attack, we have a better chance of stopping them if they ever do get a bomb," I said. "We've done it. Every one of you contributed in crucial ways to solving this mystery."

"It's been a privilege," Norman said. "So, this little team will be folded now?"

"Probably," Christine said. "Last week, I was mad to be here. Now I'm sad to see it end."

"This has been the most interesting job I've had," Tori said. "Andrew, if you need an Intelligence Analyst in your next Arabic shop, keep me in mind."

Matt's face lowered. "This was the first time I ever felt I mattered in the Agency."

Norman put his hand on Matt's shoulder. "You did great, guy. Just keep doing what you're doing."

I stood from the table. "I'm going to write up what we've discovered here. I'll attach it to Tori's report and send it to our Branch Chief, Dave. As your boss, I'm giving you the rest of the day off. In two hours, meet me back at that Mexican place. Again, I'm buying."

***

If this all sounds too easy, it was. Once again, we laughed and ate and drank and celebrated what we thought was a mission accomplished. And we were wrong.

Chapter Twelve

Friday, March 25: 2:03 AM

My phone should not be ringing at this hour! But in my line of work, I don't assume a call in the middle of the night is a wrong number.

"Yes?" I managed through a frog in my throat.

"Andrew, It's Dave. You've got to come in ASAP."

He hung up. I speed dialed Norman and told him to send the message through our calling chain. A fast shower and I was in my car driving through a moonless night. Only as I was taking the NSA exit and approaching the security gate did I notice a turmoil of nerves in my stomach. Something very big was going on. There was no other reason for calling my team in at this hour.

Despite the seeming urgency of Dave's call, I knew I would need coffee to function. And so, after a quick stop at the never-closing cafeteria, I was stepping into our office, ready for anything.

Dave was already there.

"Thanks for coming in so quickly," he said. "We've got some guests in the main conference room ready to brief us on what's going on."

"Shouldn't we wait for my team?"

He shook his head. "You didn't need to call them in. There's no time. You can fill them in later."

I followed him down the hall and into the room. A man and woman were already there and stood as we entered.

"I'm Dr. Alfred Witter, from MI-5," said the tall and slightly balding man, offering his hand to shake. "Nice to meet you, Dr. Valquist." He was wearing a brown suit that looked as if it had been worn for three days straight. I don't know fine distinctions among accents, but I could tell he was British.

"A pleasure to meet you," I returned.

The woman, blonde and just a little shorter than Witter, shook my hand. "I'm Sharon Cruze, one of the GCHQ liaisons here at NSA," she said in an accent I recognized as thoroughly Scottish.

Now, I had learned in my short time at the NSA that we enjoy a particularly close intelligence sharing relationship with the United Kingdom. GCHQ stands for Government Communication Headquarters and is the UK equivalent to the NSA. MI-5 and MI-6 are the UK agencies roughly equivalent to our CIA, with MI-5 focusing on domestic matters and MI-6 charged with foreign intelligence.

So I wasn't surprised to meet two UK officers at all. The early hour, however, still implied something extraordinary was going on.

AMOR VINCIT OMNIA

"Let's get right to business," Dave said, sitting down.

We followed his lead and Ms. Cruze set a piece of paper in front of me.

"GCHQ intercepted this through an extremely sensitive source. We do know that both the sender and recipient are known members of the Adler Group."

I read the message. "The Package is en route. Tempus Fugit."

"Add this piece of information to it," Witter said, passing me another sheet.

I saw a curious classification at the top of the page: Top Secret: Release to UK and USA/Urgent. This was a message from GRU, the Russian Main Intelligence Directorate:

> Be informed that one item of the class RA-115s has been stolen from our control. It was illegally sold to the Adlerites for a sum of several million USD. The culprit on our end has been identified and dealt with. But the item remains unaccounted for.

Under the English text was the same message in Russian. As I scanned over it, I was surprised at how little I had forgotten in the two decades since my mother had taught me that language as part of her plan to liberate Romania from the Communists.

"RA-115s?" I asked.

"Suitcase Nuke," Dave said.

"I thought those were just a myth."

"We've gone back and forth on whether to believe the defectors who first claimed they were real," Witter said. "With this report, Russia has ended all doubt."

"We've read your entire report," Ms. Cruse said. "Nice work on the acrostic. You've identified Rome as the place where they intend to strike?"

"Yes," I said. "In fact, we can even identify a specific Church in Rome that they seem to intend as their point of attack."

"It's lucky we got that book when we did," Dave said.

"Probably this isn't quite a coincidence," Witter said. "We think they've basically spent all the money they have on this weapon. And they're rushing their attack to fruition hoping to strike before you all figured out the spot."

"Then basically, this is all good news for us," Dave said. "Not only have they exhausted their resources, but they've miscalculated. We know where they're going and we'll be able to stop them."

"How do you stop them?" I asked.

"They've given me data that will let me detect the transponder on the weapon," Witter said. "So when they approach the site, we'll apprehend them."

I took a deep breath. They were talking about catching people with nuclear bombs. It didn't all sound quite as simple as they were making it out to be. "And there's no danger of them setting it off before you stop them?"

Witter turned to Dave. "You haven't told him?"

"I haven't had time."

"Tell me what?" I asked.

"You're going to Rome as a part of the response team."

"The RA-115s can only be set to go off on a timer," Dr. Witter said. "After we neutralize the person transporting the weapon, you'll be patched in with a technician at the GRU to defuse the thing before it goes off."

"Why me?"

"We were told you know Russian."

"Yes, but does this have to be done in Russian?"

"It actually does," Dave said. "GRU says no one in that program knows adequate English to talk someone through this process safely."

"And there's no way we try this through a translator," Ms. Cruze said.

"We're pretty sure they'll be moving this device on the ground," Witter said. "That means we do have a full day before we should expect the arrival of the weapon. That's plenty of time to get in place."

I sat back and absorbed all this information. My heart was pounding in a combination of the coffee I had just slammed down and the realization that millions of lives would depend on me.

***

I had just finished telling my team everything I had learned. Even deep within the building, we could hear the low thud of helicopter rotors approaching the roof above us. That was my ride.

Dave poked his head into our office from the hallway outside. "We're heading up to the roof in just a minute. Get ready to go."

"Yes, sir," I said.

As the door closed again, I had a strange feeling. And for a reason I did not understand, I turned them into words.

"I don't like that man," I said.

"What's wrong, Andrew?" Christine asked.

"I don't know. It just seems like he's been pulling the carpet out from under me since the moment I met him."

"We're all tired," Tori said. "But I agree with you. I've worked under many fine men and women in this Agency. He's not among them."

"It bothers me that he didn't want you all included in that briefing," I continued. "This isn't all about me. I could not have done any of this without all of you."

"With all due respect," Norman said. "We've moved beyond that. They need you for skills that only you can bring now. And I'm just proud to have worked with someone so important in this moment."

"Good luck," said a teary-eyed Matt, stepping toward me and stretching out his hand.

"That won't do it," I said, wrapping my arms around him.

One by one I hugged each of them, who in turn then shared embraces.

"When I get back, we're all going out to eat again," I said, wiping away tears.

"Except this time, you aren't buying," Christine said.

***

The helicopter took us to a small jet at Andrews Air Force Base. Dave, Dr. Witter, and I were soon over the Atlantic. I closed my eyes but found no sleep.

***

"Who's in charge of the team in Dr. Valquist's absence?" Christine asked.

"I assume Norman," Tori said. "He's the QC'er, and that's the ranking position."

"No way!" Norman protested. "This is on the basis of seniority. Tori, you've been in the military longer than me, you've been at the Agency longer than all of us. It's obviously you."

"Well it sure isn't me," Matt said. "I say we put it up to a vote. All in favor of Tori being in charge?"

"Aye!" said Norman, Matt, and Christine.

"Then it's decided," Christine said. "Tori, it's almost 3 AM. Can you please send us home to go back to sleep?"

Tori laughed. "Sorry, people. We all have to put in eight hours today. And we've already put in one. We may as well consider ourselves on the clock and just get through it."

"Alright," Christine said, sitting down at her work station. "Give us our orders."

"Christine," Tori started. "You spend the next seven hours studying your Arabic. You're going to get called back into that service any minute anyway. Norman, you double check the book for any residual typos. Matt, you memorize all the quotes in that final chapter. They're apparently important things to know."

"What are you going to do?" Matt asked.

"I need to chase down a loose thread called Dave." She fired up her computer and started to work.

***

By six in the morning, the surrounding teams were starting to arrive at their workstations. The four continued their duties, heading toward the midpoint of their work day.

"I like this one," Matt said aloud. "*Amor tussisque non celantur*."

"Love and a cough cannot be hidden," Christine translated instinctively.

"I forget," Norman said, continuing to type out a grammatical note into the manuscript. "Where does that one appear?"

"It's the "*A*" of the *Amor* in *Sero te Amor*," Matt said, suddenly chuckling. "Have you ever noticed that *Amor* is *Roma* backwards?"

Norman stopped typing.

Christine slowly pushed away from her workstation.

"What's going on, people?" Tori asked, sensing a deep and sudden tension in the air.

"Damn," Norman whispered.

"Quick," Christine said. "Write it out."

Tori stood and walked toward them. "Is there a problem?"

Norman copied the acrostic backwards as Christine looked over his shoulder. They both gasped.

"What's going on?!" Tori shouted.

"The whole thing is a palindrome," Norman said.

'What's that?" Matt asked.

"It reads in each direction," Christine replied. "Here's what the acrostic says if we read it backward. AULA STAT SACRA BIS IN SECUNDA ROMA ET ORES."

"The palace stands sacred twice," Norman translated. "In the second Rome. And may you pray."

"Is there any way this is a pure coincidence?" Tori asked.

Christine shook her head. "Absolutely not. We've made a huge mistake."

Tori put her head in her hands. "I've been sending out messages to everyone who's ever worked with Dave. And no one likes him and no one trusts him."

"What's the point?" Matt asked.

"He never asked us if we were sure about our conclusion," Norman said. "It's like he wanted that Church in Rome to be the final word."

"And we now know that it was wrong," Matt said. "So you mean he knew we were wrong?"

"I get it," Tori said. "He's one of them. And it makes sense. They got their power from placing people in important positions."

Matt stood up and formed angry fists. "Putting a man inside the NSA office tasked with fighting the Adler Group was the perfect play."

"But where's the actual attack site?" Tori asked.

Christine and Norman looked at each other. "Istanbul," they said together.

"Constantinople was known as the Second Rome," Norman said.

"Okay, people," Tori said. "Andrew is on his way to Rome with a member of the Adler Group. And we have no way to get in touch with him. And a Suitcase Nuke seems to be on its way to Istanbul. Any ideas?"

Norman clenched his eyes shut. "*Oremus.* Let us pray."

Chapter Thirteen

Friday, March 25: 6:04 AM

"Let's hear the options, people," Norman said.

"What if we told Dave's boss about our suspicions?" Matt asked.

"Very risky," Christine replied. "Dave might not be the only one in management who's in on this. The best thing would be somehow letting Andrew know without getting anyone else involved."

"Agreed," Tori stated. "Except for the fact that we have no way to contact him. What about Witter, the MI-5 agent on the mission? Could a GCHQ liaison here at NSA contact him for us?"

Christine shook her head. "Same problem as our management. If Witter's also in on it, it's a disaster."

Matt raised his hand.

"Yes?" Norman asked.

"Even if we could somehow contact Andrew, that's just the beginning of his problems. He's still on a mission with at least one Adlerite. He's got no resources and no connections over there."

"Let's solve the first crisis first," Tori said.

"His brother," Matt said, starting to smile.

The group all turned to him.

"What do you mean?" Christine asked.

"Andrew's made all kinds of references to talking to his twin brother almost daily," he explained. "When he gets to Rome, he'll call Stefan and talk to him."

"But Andrew won't have his cell phone on him," Tori said.

"He'll find a way," Matt countered. "We need to get Stefan in on this."

"You're talking about revealing classified information to someone without the proper clearance," Norman said.

"There's no other choice," Tori said.

"I agree," he said. "And I'm going to take responsibility for all of it." Norman reached onto his desk and picked up his garrison cap. "I'm going to my car for a few minutes."

Christine smiled. "You have a smart phone there, right?"

"Yes. I'll find his number on his parish website, I'm sure. Can't make that call from an unclassified phone here anyway, because…"

"We don't know whether an Adlerite is monitoring our team to make sure we haven't figured this all out," Matt stated. "What are you going to tell him?"

Norman smiled faintly. "I'm going to tell him everything."

***

AMOR VINCIT OMNIA

Our flight across the Atlantic had been much slower than my trip on the SR-71 the previous week. But what we gave up in speed, we gained in comfort. The main cabin of this private jet was set up as a veritable lounge. Witter and Dave sat across from me in plush dark brown leather reclining seats. An attendant had served us meals worthy of any first class cabin and kept our wine glasses full of selections far outside my normal price range. As I sat sipping from my glass, somewhere over the British Isles, I wondered over just how well Witter and Dave knew each other. They seemed familiar enough that they might be great old friends, or maybe one or both are just the type of people to warm to strangers quickly.

I dribbled a bit of wine from my glass onto the serving tray over my lap, remembering a special time my twin brother Stefan and I had prayed for our departed ancestors with the gesture.

"*Pentru morți,*" Witter said softly, noticing what I had done.

I looked up a bit startled that he would know, not just the tradition, but the Romanian version of the phrase 'For the Dead'.

He smiled. "I was stationed in Bucharest for a few months, Dr. Valquist. And I always try to go native as much as the mission will allow."

"What's this about?" Dave asked.

"Romanian Orthodox like Dr. Valquist sometimes pray for their dead with a sort of wine offering. I'm certain it goes back to ancient Roman practices."

"You're probably right," I said, now sipping from the glass. "So what's the plan when we land? When should the RA-115s be arriving at the site?"

"No way to know for sure," Dave said. "But it should be within a day. We'll arrive at 2 PM local time and move immediately to the Basilica, where we'll set up an inconspicuous watch just outside."

"There's a narrow street which runs along the main entrance," I said, recalling the site from memory of a previous trip. "It's a busy enough area that three men loitering in the courtyard in front shouldn't seem out of place."

"Good plan," Witter said. "Based on assumptions of over the road travel from Russia, if they don't come this evening, they'll certainly arrive tomorrow."

I nodded, actually pretending to understand the scenario better than I did. My mind was still awhirl from this sudden and serious mission. The alcohol of the wine was actually clearing my head a bit. The attendant seemed to read this and refilled my glass.

A few hours later, we landed at a private airport just outside Rome. A black SUV was waiting for us on the tarmac and soon we were speeding toward the Basilica of Saint Augustine, just East of the Tiber River. I put my hand instinctively to my left shirt pocket to feel for my cell phone.

Witter again noticed my action. "Who do you want to call?" he asked, reaching into his coat pocket.

I locked eyes with my boss. "Would it be okay to call my twin brother?"

"Do you talk a lot?"

"Every day. He probably called me today and wonders where I am."

"No problem," he said. "Nothing classified, of course."

"Is my location classified?"

"No," Dave replied. "Just the mission."

Witter handed over the phone. "Just dial it direct," he said. "Her Majesty's Special Service will pick up the tab."

I chuckled and took the device. "Thanks."

After I dialed the number and heard the ring tone, I worried for an instant that Stefan probably wouldn't pick up if he saw some strange number calling.

"Hello, Andrew," I heard, and immediately wondered how he would know it was me.

"Good morning, Stefan," I said. "I mean, it's still morning for you. I'm in Rome. I had the last minute opportunity to go on a free trip for a few days."

"That's awesome!" he said. "I just *looove* Roma."

His emphasis on the word *love* was an effect I had never heard my twin ever before make. I know my brother well enough to know that something very strange was going on.

"I'll be back in a few days," I continued. "I just wanted to call quick and let you know so you wouldn't worry if you called me at home."

"No problem," he said. "Make sure you go the Forum and see the Temple of Pollux and Castor."

My blood froze. He had spoken the code names our mother gave us when she trained us to fight as insurgents against communist Romania. And he had mentioned them in the reverse order of how they are usually stated.

"Alright, Stefan," I said, knowing that he had just somehow told me something very important. "I'll call you when I get back."

"*Te iubesc*," Stefan whispered. "*Ai grijă de tine.*"

I closed the phone and handed it back to Witter.

"Everything alright?" Dave asked.

"Fine," I said, feigning a smile, my mind racing to figure out what had just happened.

Stefan had definitely just sent me a coded message. I quickly thought through the data points. The word love. He *loooves* Rome. No, not quite. He had said he *loooves* Roma. And our code names means he knows

I'm actually right now in battle. But why mention the names backwards?

Love

Roma

Backwards

What does it all mean?

And then it struck me. *Amor*, love, is *Roma* backwards. A strange calm settled upon my heart as I reversed the acrostic and figured out both the new message and why Stefan must know about it. The team had clearly figured out the reverse message and felt they needed to tell me. I was also instantly aware that the implication of us racing to Rome at Dave's insistence was that he knew it was the wrong site. Dave was an Adlerite. That somehow all now made perfect sense. The team figured that out as well. So telling Stefan about this, knowing I would call him, was a brilliant solution. Except now, I still didn't have any good way to respond to my new predicament. I was on a mission to stop a nuclear bomb in Rome, only the real bomb will be set off in Istanbul. My boss, sitting right across from me, knows all this. He's the one, I presume, with a gun, not to mention a way to tell the other Adlerites if I just bolt from the team and try to go stop the real bomb. How would I even try to stop the real bomb if I safely got away from him? Would I go to the airport and try to buy a plane ticket? Istanbul could be gone before I arrived. Was Witter in on this as well? Probably not, but I couldn't take the chance he was and bring him in on my side.

I had figured everything out. And I had virtually no good options. I did the only thing left. I prayed and waited to see if somehow my current situation might change.

"It's just another block," the driver said toward us.

"Thanks," I replied. Through the front windshield I recognized the neighborhood. The next cross street would be one block west of a narrow gate which formed an enclosed courtyard housing the basilica.

"As we get out, just walk with me casually," Dave said. "We're tourists on vacation."

Witter had briefed me that his smart phone contained a number of added features, including the ability to detect the bomb's transponder from the info the Russians had supplied. It would let us know when the bomb was a within a mile, as well give us a firm direction on the device.

The car stopped and we stepped out the side doors. I stretched my arms high in the air. My mother had taught me to prepare for any potential action by loosening my body well. Since I knew that bomb was not really coming this way, I would eventually be forced to do something to get away from this ruse. But at the moment, I needed to play along with our mission until I figured out the best plan of action.

I followed the two men through the gate and saw the steps leading to the basilica on our left. The white marble facade of the building shone brilliantly down from a high set of steps leading to the main entrance. I instinctively turned toward the structure and made the sign of the cross. And as I looked up, I saw her face. There at the top of the stairs, leaning against the front wall of the church stood Aurora. Our eyes met for just a moment. She winked and looked away.

"Nothing yet," Witter said, pretending to text on his phone.

"Could I go up and visit the Church?" I asked. "It's more suspicious for a tourist to not enter than to stand down here indefinitely."

Dave chuckled. "Sure. No problem. Keep it short, just in case Witter gets a reading."

"Yeah," the British officer said. "If I pick something up, it would mean they're maybe five to ten minutes away."

"I'll be right back."

I turned and walked toward the bottom of the stairs. As I started up, I looked and saw that Aurora was gone from her previous spot. She would have anticipated my request to visit the inside and gone ahead.

I pulled against the tall double doors and found them heavy and sluggish to open. Stepping inside, I found the interior brighter than expected. The tall stone ceiling stretched the long sanctuary toward an ornate high altar against the distant wall. Aurora stood facing me to my left.

"You've never been to Rome before, right?" I asked softly.

"No," she replied in a whisper.

"There's a work by Caravaggio and Raphael in this Church."

"I read about it on the plane. And the high altar has an icon painted by Saint Luke himself."

"I'm in serious trouble, Aurora. I assume Stefan called you?"

She nodded. "This is all connected to that book?"

"And one of the men outside on my team is an enemy."

"I'm not here officially, Andrew," she said. "But I've got the resources to do what you need. What's your plan?"

"We need to escape from here and get to Istanbul."

"That's doable," she said. "But not if we're being pursued."

I knew what she was saying. Dave at least had to be out of commission. "Understood."

"A block north on Via dell'Orso you'll see a white car, Romanian diplomatic plates. I'll be ready to race as soon as you're in. I'll have a jet waiting for us at the airport."

"You're out on a limb for me again."

"Romania needs you to succeed, right?"

I smiled. "The whole world needs me to succeed. See you in a few minutes."

She quickly went out through the doors.

I turned toward the main altar and crossed myself three times. In mere seconds my mind raced through two thousand years of theological discourse on the topic of the Just War. While our Savior had taught us to turn the other cheek, killing in self-defense is ultimately justifiable from the level of the individual all the way up to nation states. In this particular case, however, taking out Dave meant preemptively defending millions from what his group intended. The numbers alone might convince some that this was a no-brainer. But I wished there was something I could do to immobilize him short of outright taking his life. I mean, despite my certainty about the situation, was there any possibility I was simply wrong?

The faces of all the men whose lives I had taken swirled before my mind's eye. The man back in Bucharest a few days earlier. Several men in Romania when Stefan and I had visited last year. Five men in

Iraq. And inside me now something grieved to imagine that I was not done killing. But I knew what this moment required of me. I would walk out of this Church and strike Dave in the face with enough force that I would immobilize him for at least a day. And there was no way to do that without using an amount of energy capable of also taking his life. If I struck with less, he might yet foil my attempt to stop that bomb. As for Witter, I would take Dave's gun and turn it on him. I would tell the Brit that I can't trust him but I would risk leaving him out of it. I might be wrong. Witter might be an Adlerite as well. But without any evidence, force directed against him would just be murder.

And I prayed the prayer passed down through my family, whenever we would go into battle. "Forgive me, Lord, that I must take life precious to you." I crossed myself and walked out of the Church.

As I came down the steps, Dave could not have seen anything suspicious in my gait. Because what I was about to do was nowhere in my thoughts. This was a trick I learned from my mother. I was returning to my boss after a short visit in the Church. And I was about to ask him where I should station myself next.

"Nice visit to your God?" Dave asked.

I smiled and in the next second my fist drove through his left eye. I heard and felt a crunch of bone and knew that my blow had likely exceeded the necessary force. He was on his back and my hand slipped into his suit pocket. I retrieved his pistol.

"Whoa!" Witter hollered.

As I stood and turned toward him, I saw that the Brit already had his pistol drawn on me.

"Dave is an Adlerite," I said calmly, pointing Dave's gun into Witter's face. "I'm leaving here to stop the bomb. I can't trust you, and I need you to give me that magic phone of yours."

"What's your evidence?" he asked, carefully handing over the device.

"It doesn't matter," I said. A commotion of people built around us from the sight of the fallen Dave.

"I can't just let you bolt!"

"Then you're going to have to shoot me," I said, putting the pistol and phone in my jacket. I walked quickly north. Picking up my pace toward a full run, I reached the Via Dell'Orso. Scanning quickly in each direction, I saw a number of white cars, but the bright blue diplomatic plates stood out a few yards to my left.

I jumped in the passenger side. "Go!"

Aurora slammed on the accelerator. "I'd like to have just one year of my life when you and I don't have to race to save the world."

Chapter Fourteen

Friday, March 25: 6:33 PM

The gentle rhythm of the waves caressing the shore ahead touched my heart with a welcome peace. I soaked up strength from the moment, recalling our race from Rome to this point. During just a ten minute drive to the airport, I had told Aurora every detail left of the current mission. Flashes of memory from there put us on a plane. Then we were in Constanţa, at the same military base where I had landed the previous week. A helicopter ride over the Black Sea dropped us onto a boat perfectly camouflaged as a Turkish fishing vessel. The Romanian Intelligence Service certainly knows how to operate in their corner of the world. And now, we were pulling up to a dock a few miles north of Istanbul proper.

"This is as far as the boat dares to take us," Aurora said. "An embassy car will be waiting for us there."

We waited for what seemed an eternity as dock attendants secured the vessel with ropes and a gangway was lowered. Our vehicle, a dark green sedan with little Romanian flags on the four corners, was idling just off the dock. Both rear doors opened for us. We piled in and soon we were again on the move.

As we moved south on an urban highway, my thoughts drifted even further back into all the events that led up to this point. A year earlier I had just gotten back from Iraq and then been on an unexpected adventure with my twin. And there I had fallen in love with Aurora. Then Aurora broke us off, since her high position within the SRI did not allow her to be in a relationship with a non-Romanian citizen. Then I was applying for the NSA. Then I was inside and actually hoping for a quiet desk job doing whatever an Arabic linguist at the NSA does there (of which I was still largely in the dark). Then came a mission to steal a book from a library—a mission that managed to become a fire fight. Then came a welcome lull in the action in which I brushed up on my Latin in what should have been a purely academic exercise. And now, after all I had been through, I was minutes away from a do or die interception of a nuclear bomb.

"Any idea of where exactly to expect this thing?" she asked, jarring me out of my thoughts.

"Symbolically the old city is as good a guess as any."

And then we both heard a beep from my coat pocket. I took out Witter's phone and saw a red screen.

Aurora leaned over. "Good news, I hope?"

RA-115s detected, we both read.

"Yes and no," she said.

"We're led to believe that the device can only be set to go off on an hour-long timer," I noted. "This is a failsafe to give the bomber time to theoretically get a safe distance away."

"At least the old Soviets weren't suicide bombers," she said. "And they probably will wait until they are in place to set the timer."

I nodded. We're about a mile north of the old city. I'm going to bet they're already there."

Aurora leaned forward. "Driver, if you're not already going as fast as possible, it's time to start."

As we continued, an arrow appeared on the display confirming my theory about the detonation point. I saw the famous dome of Hagia Sophia rise over the neighboring buildings. This impressive structure had started as the crown jewel of Eastern Churches, then was turned into a mosque, and now is a museum. The direction finder pointed to the large park just southwest of the building. The display indicated a distance of just a hundred feet.

"Stop here," I said.

We were out of the car and walking casually together, looking down at the display and up toward the sprawling green park, centered with a large circular pool. Just about where the device indicated, we saw three men seated on a bench with a large suitcase at their feet.

"That's them," Aurora whispered.

"Agreed. Do they have back-up?"

We swept the scene with eyes expert for where a defensive grid should be placed.

"One man stationed twenty meters at five o'clock from their position," she said.

"Got him. And another past the bench by twenty meters." I shook my head. "Even if we rush this scene and shoot to kill, we're not taking control of that bomb."

"If only you had one more shooter," a voice said behind us.

We turned quickly. And there stood Witter smiling.

"How did you get here?" I asked.

"I've been here an hour," he said. "I had no choice but to assume you were right about Dave, so from there I figured out the reverse message. He's going to live, in case you were wondering."

"I'm relieved," I said.

"So why haven't you stopped them?" Aurora asked.

"By myself? Besides, we still need the Russian to talk Andrew through the disarming. Here's my plan, I'm walking a hundred meters ten o'clock. Then, I double back, shooting the far look out. I arrive at the bench and help mop up if you two haven't gotten all of the rest."

AMOR VINCIT OMNIA

I locked eyes with Aurora. "At this point we have no choice but to trust him."

"And his plan's as good as any."

"Let's do it, Witter. What's the signal?"

"When you see me start to run, you move."

"Got it."

We stood watching the scene as Witter walked into the park.

"I think we're at the point in this mission where we might as well bring the Turks in for final help," she said.

"You're right," I returned. "Can you make that happen?"

Aurora was already on her phone, speaking with some SRI element in Istanbul. She closed the device. "Turkish intelligence is about to be alerted. They'll be here in time to keep things clear."

I saw that Witter was approaching the spot from which he would stage his next move. In my peripheral vision, I spotted Aurora making the sign of the cross.

"On your mark, Castor," she said.

I chuckled to hear my code name. "You go wide right, Minerva," I said, with the code name she had received from my uncle. You take out the five o'clock and then turn in to help."

Witter began to run. We bolted forward. As we ran toward the assembled opponents, I saw them all notice our approach and begin to move. All I could do was deal with the men on the bench and hope Witter and Aurora took care of the outer guards. I drew my gun as I continued forward. They were still farther away than I wanted to begin firing, but I could not risk them scattering out of my control. One of them reached down and grabbed the suitcase. I stopped and shot. He spun around and fell; I continued forward. Another of them raised his gun and aimed it at a point Aurora would be nearing. I fired without stopping and saw him crumble.

I heard other shots and hoped they were coming from Witter and Aurora taking out their targets and not the other way around.

The third man on the bench dove to the ground and scooped up the suitcase. He was running away from me. I raised my gun, hating the notion of shooting him in the back, but hating more his escape. A shot fired before me and the man fell.

"Saved you the moral ambiguity, chap," Witter said, arriving at my left.

"Mission accomplished," Aurora said, running up.

Dozens of police whistles were descending on the area. A group of plain clothed men were running in our direction from the main street.

"Romanian agents, identify!" screamed one of them, holding up a badge.

"Romanians, here!" Aurora shouted back, raising her hands.

Witter handed me a phone. "You're now on the line with the Russian bomb expert. Move fast, I just hope there's time."

"*Da*?" I said, sitting on the grass and pulling the suitcase toward me. I looked at Witter. "Where'd you get another phone?"

"I carry four at all times," he said.

Following the Russian's directions, I opened the suitcase. We all gasped to see a glowing red LCD counting down a final thirty seconds.

"Holy Mary, Mother of God!" I blurted. I imagined the disarmament process would involve removal of components and cutting of wires. And there was just no time.

"What number do you see on the lower left of the display?" the Russian said quickly.

"5639," I shot out.

"Get ready to enter the cancellation code," I heard on the other end.

A ton lifted from me. "Go!"

One by one I carefully pressed a series of numbers he stated. The countdown continued. Fifteen, fourteen, thirteen... and then it stopped.

I sat back. No words were spoken as the three of us processed what had taken place.

Finally Aurora dropped down next to me. Witter followed.

"You just saved the world, Dr. Valquist," he said.

Chapter Fifteen

Monday, March 28: 9:00 AM

"On behalf of the United States," the General began, "I extend our sincere gratitude to you two, Agent Aurora Zamfir and Agent Alfred Witter. I've been authorized to present you both with the Secretary of Defense Medal for Outstanding Public Service."

"Congratulations, you two," I said.

"It's the highest award the Department of Defense can give to non-US citizens," the General said, standing and opening a blue velvet box.

He pinned the medals on Aurora and Witter and shook their hands.

After everyone had taken their seats, the General looked at me and smiled.

"Let me guess," I said. "No medal for me because I was on the clock?"

He chuckled. "Essentially. If you were still in the military, this thing would have gotten you the Congressional Medal of Honor. But the only medals I could give you explicitly recognize *years* of service. And they tell me today's your two week anniversary at the Agency."

"That's alright, sir. I ask only one thing. My team, Sergeants Valley and Brandt, Matthew Gallings, Christine…"

"Have all been given promotions in their rank or pay scale. As have you, Dr. Valquist. And they've all been told they can pick their next assignment from the entire Department of Defense enterprise."

"Good."

"And so," the Director said, "this final debriefing is complete. Agents Zamfir and Witter, your helicopter is waiting on the roof. Dr. Valquist, your team, I've been told, is expecting you back at your office. They say you're all going out to eat and this time it's their treat?"

He shook my hand firmly and smiled, his eyes now welling with tears. "God bless you," he said. "Something tells me I'll be seeing you again."

"Thank you, sir," I replied. "It's an honor to serve."

The General walked out, followed by three uniformed attendants.

"Be well, Dr. Valquist," Witter said, shaking my hand. "Don't get too comfortable. Turns out our governments think we work well together. I'll be seeing you very soon."

"When were they going to tell me about this?"

"Welcome to government service." He walked out of the room.

And once again, I was alone with Aurora.

AMOR VINCIT OMNIA

"Listen, Aurora. I've decided I want that casual contact."

She looked at me startled. In her eyes I saw a sudden worry. And then they flooded with tears. "Do you mean..."

"Do I mean I don't love you anymore and just want to be friends?" I laughed out loud. "No, Agent Zamfir, that has not changed." I put my hands on her shoulders. "But if I can't have you in my life in that way, I want anything else we can still share."

"This won't be easy."

"It'll be easier than saving the world." I leaned over and kissed her on the forehead. "Call me when you get home. Stefan has my number."

She sobbed and then smiled. Turning around, she walked out of the room. As I saw her long blonde hair swirl away, I leaned over and drew in a breath of the air in which her perfume still lingered.

"I love you, Aurora Zamfir," I whispered. "And I probably always will."

Printed in Great Britain
by Amazon

21168932R00088